MIDNIGHT in Park City

HOPE HOLLOWAY

AND

CECELIA SCOTT

Midnight in Park City

Christmas in the Canyons Book 4

Hope Holloway and Cecelia Scott

Copyright © 2025 Hope Holloway

Christmas in the Canyons

Sleigh Bells in Park City
Snowfall in Park City
Mistletoe in Park City
Midnight in Park City

Chapter One
MJ

Was that George? George McBride, her beloved husband?

Why did he look like a twenty-five-year-old man, striding across the field behind Snowberry Lodge in a soft flannel and worn jeans, moving with that understated but manly swagger earned from years of hard work and clean living?

Transported forty years into the past, MJ feasted her eyes on the man she'd married who was definitely *not* the same middle-aged George she'd tearfully buried six years ago.

Wait. Was he...singing?

No, no, he was whistling. Blowing out that melody she knew so well. She recognized the lilting notes of Louis Armstrong on a scratchy record player in their bedroom, and remembered dancing in their pajamas after the baby fell asleep.

Just the two of them, singing about...*trees of green... red roses, too...*and...*what a wonderful world.*

"It's always going to be our song, MJ," he called out to her, holding up a hand as the whistling got louder and louder. "Nobody else's, sweetheart! Just you and me, forever."

He whistled the crescendo of the song, the notes high-pitched. They no longer sounded like a human but a digital beeping. Or was that—

MJ's eyes popped open, then she blinked, lost and confused, surrounded by a pitch-black room, her heart hammering, her palms damp, her soul aching for... George. Young George. Her George. Her one and only...

"It was a dream," she groaned as the realization hit.

Then she sat up straighter, not trusting her own ears.

"Then why do I still hear the music?"

Shocked by the distant but distinct melody, she threw back her comforter and let her bare feet hit the warm rug over hardwood floors. Taking a breath, she reached for her robe at the bottom of the bed, then stood, frowning and disoriented.

That song!

Why was it playing? Where was it...

She flexed her fingers and wiggled her toes. Totally awake, so this wasn't part of her dream.

A recurring dream, she acknowledged, about her late husband. He was always in the back behind Snowberry Lodge, coming from her mother's old garden, a tool or two dangling from his hand, their favorite song on his lips as he whistled.

But this dream had audible music and...*it hadn't stopped!*

She reached to the lamp on her nightstand, turning on the light to spill a golden glow around the bedroom.

As soon as she did, the music stopped.

Okay. It was a dream. Just a vivid, wonderful, unexpected dream.

Slightly shaken, MJ pulled her robe over her arms and belted it, longing for something to make her feel steady and secure.

"Oh, George." She rubbed the fleece sleeves, giving in to a shiver that she hoped would shake off a dream she hadn't had in, oh, almost a year.

In fact, she realized, she hadn't dreamed about George...since she'd met Matt.

Sighing, she walked to her phone charging on the dresser and tapped it to see it was a few minutes past three. She normally rose with no alarm at five, so there wasn't much point in trying to go back to sleep.

She eyed the bed, which looked warm and inviting and...empty.

Now that Matt Walker had arrived at Snowberry Lodge, keeping a written promise he'd made a year ago, did MJ need to think about her bed *not* being empty?

The only man she'd ever shared a bed with was...the handsome one in her dreams whistling *What a Wonderful World*.

Would that change now that Matt had returned to Park City?

"Slow down there, girlfriend," she whispered to herself. "He only came back last night."

But, oh, had he come back. Just hours ago, as she danced at her sister's wedding—Cindy's remarriage to her ex-husband had been a glorious event—MJ's totally girlish fantasies had come true.

Girlish because she was sixty-three, but the moment was no less...fantastic.

On the dance floor with her father, MJ had turned to look into the eyes and fall into the arms of the man who'd disappeared almost a year ago, leaving behind a letter promising he'd be back in a year.

Oh, and he'd also left a million-dollar gift to Snowberry Lodge that had been used for a massive renovation of the family's property on the outskirts of Park City.

The letter said he'd come back after he gave away most of the multimillion-dollar lottery winnings that had changed his life, since that kind of wealth had caused him more unhappiness than one would imagine.

That promise had given MJ many sleepless nights, a thousand imagined scenarios, and the highest of high hopes.

Despite being a lifelong optimist, MJ had many days of doubt. She'd never heard from him in that year—not a single word. But he'd asked for time, space, and a chance to manage the responsibility of all that money.

Then, last night, when he tapped her father's shoulder and cut into their dance, every doubt disappeared and she'd let herself feel the first real giddy, breathless, unbelievable stirrings of love.

No wonder she'd dreamed about George...and heard their song.

Standing for a moment in the chilly room, she gave up on sleep. Instead, she'd have a nice morning tea by her fire and could be in the kitchen early to prepare a post-wedding breakfast for the guests who'd stayed last night.

Satisfied with that decision, she stepped into slippers and went into the living room, turning on a light and looking around at the peaceful and warm home she'd created.

She never tired of the owner's suite apartment that sat atop Snowberry Lodge's rambling main building. After George's passing, she'd left the big house on the edge of the property where they'd lived together. Her father, Red, along with her daughter and grandson, lived there now.

She'd moved into the staff "quarters"—basically a glorified bedroom and bath—off the lodge's main kitchen. That had helped with her grief when George died, and made running Snowberry's kitchen easy and convenient.

When they received the windfall of Matt's cash a year ago, she and Cindy had a vision to transform the unused third floor into a beautiful apartment. Yes, it could be rented out for top dollar, but Cindy had insisted that MJ make it her home. After all, it was MJ's friendship with Matt that provided the money that essentially saved their family business.

MJ agreed and had designed the space exactly for her needs. The bedroom was roomy but still cozy, with a luxurious ensuite and a dreamy soaker tub where she frequently ended her long days. The living area was spacious and bathed in natural light, with a nicely equipped kitchenette, a breakfast nook, and a gorgeous stone fireplace she'd watched a talented mason build by hand.

From the soft, dusty blue curtains to the braided rugs to the soul-soothing view of the Wasatch mountain peaks, MJ had made this sanctuary the perfect home for a sixty-three-year-old widow.

But would all that change with Matt's return? Her home, her marital status, her whole life?

With a sigh of both hope and uncertainty, she filled a kettle and started a fire, humming *What a Wonderful World* the whole time.

"Goodness, that sounded real," she mused, thinking about the melody in her dreams. "It sounded just like…"

Her music box!

She froze in the act of pouring scalding water into a cup, realizing with a start that she had no idea where her treasured music box was. Still up in the house where she'd lived with George? No, she'd never leave that behind.

She couldn't recall the last time she'd laid eyes on that music box, though, which was sad. Surely she'd packed it when she left the house and moved in down-stairs. She couldn't remember seeing it when she moved to this apartment.

Good heavens, had she lost the music box George had given her when Gracie was born?

Dropping a tea bag into the hot water, she walked back to her bedroom and looked around, scanning the bookshelves, the dresser, a few drawers, even her jewelry case where it could fit in the bottom.

Nope. Maybe it was jammed into a box she'd yet to unpack and left on the top shelf in her closet.

She peered at the storage containers, not relishing the idea of getting a stepstool and dragging them down. Still, that had to be where the music box was. For some reason, it had started playing in the middle of the night.

Unlikely...but not impossible.

Taking her tea to the chair by the fire, she thought about the gold and enamel treasure that George had given her the day that Gracie was born. The Louis Armstrong classic it played had so much meaning for them—they'd danced to it at their wedding and George loved to sing it when they were alone.

When Gracie was a baby, MJ would open the box and sing the lyrics she knew by heart while rocking her sweet daughter to sleep. George used to say the song reminded him of MJ and her deeply positive outlook on life.

She couldn't disagree—the lyrics certainly celebrated the simple, good things in life and seemed to capture how MJ liked to look at the world.

But how could it just start playing?

Maybe the dream was...*a message.*

She inhaled sharply at the thought. Maybe George had made that music box play from wherever it was as a soft whisper to...*be careful.* Or maybe he was saying she shouldn't fall for a new man at all.

Maybe George, who'd had infinite wisdom when alive and was undoubtedly in heaven with a bird's-eye view of her life, didn't think a romance with Matt was a good idea.

Now *that* tilted her world a little bit.

Yes, she'd ached for Matt to keep his promise and come back to Park City, but now that he had...what would happen? She hadn't really thought it through.

Finishing the tea, she stood to dress for the day, making a mental note to dig through the kitchen cabinets and her buffets in the guest dining area. Maybe she'd mistakenly tucked it in the wrong place.

But if she had...then what had she heard in her dream?

"Your imagination," she told herself.

Unless...it was George. She might not like what he had to say but, dead or alive, there was no one she respected or trusted more than George McBride.

So if he was talking, she knew she had to listen.

"Good morning, Mary Jane."

MJ gasped when she walked into the still-dark lodge kitchen and heard a voice from the table—and smelled coffee.

"Matt!" She froze in place, not expecting to see him before the sun rose.

"I'm still on East Coast time," he explained, pushing up from his chair. "And I knew you'd be down here before anyone else."

She watched him take a few steps closer, still getting used to seeing him in person, not her imagination. In real life, he was even taller, his chestnut hair clipped short and neat, his soft brown eyes full of nothing but warmth, his strong arms reaching for her.

With the echo of George's song in her head, she hugged him back, but resisted a kiss or a squeeze.

"You okay this morning?" he asked as he drew back, proving that he was tall, good-looking, *and* perceptive.

"Yes, I'm..." She laughed. "Still reeling."

"Why are you surprised?" he asked, searching her face. "I made you a promise."

"But I never heard boo from you."

He leaned closer, almost close enough for a kiss, and whispered, "Boo. Do you want your morning tea? I know you can't start a proper day without it."

She laughed softly, touched that he remembered her habits. "Actually, I was up very early and had some. I could use a coffee now, and company while I make breakfast for the lodge guests."

"I didn't think Snowberry Lodge was open yet," he said, walking to her coffee pot with a shocking amount of familiarity. Yes, he'd spent plenty of time in here, helping her and chatting from Thanksgiving to New Year's Eve. But it had been a different kitchen then, and a year had passed.

"We're not officially open for business yet," she told him. "But we had family and friends who traveled for the wedding and are staying, though most are leaving today. Jack's mom is staying through the holidays, though."

"Are Jack and Cindy taking a honeymoon?" he asked.

"Europe in the spring," she told him. "First of all, their daughter, Nicole, is marrying Cameron Hale on New Year's Eve."

"Yes, I heard that last night. Exciting."

She nodded. "We're happy for her. Of course, with Jack managing the lodge and filling up the newly renovated suites and cabins, my sister is focused on building the wedding business for the new Starling Room." She let a smile pull. "All of this, I might add, made possible by a lottery winner from Florida who granted wishes and won our hearts."

"Oooh, hearts have been won. That's what this 'lottery winner from Florida' likes to hear."

As she started to bring out bowls and ingredients for her pancakes, she chuckled. "You're much more than that, Matt. Oh. Can I call you Matt still? I doubt I could start calling you 'Graham' now."

Graham Matthew Walker had used his middle name when he'd stayed here, and had paid in cash. At the time, MJ had been a little suspicious—not as much as Cindy—then learned he hadn't used his full name so she couldn't Google him and find out he was worth twenty-five million in lottery winnings.

"Actually, I like it so I'm keeping it. In Utah, I'm Matt. Graham is old Florida me. And my nephew Wade will just have to deal. Oh..." He eyed her. "You're okay that he tagged along, right?"

"Of course!"

"Good, good," he said. "We're close and he's the only

relative in my circle who didn't suddenly become a different person when they found out I smelled of way too much money. We were together over Thanksgiving at his mom's house—my sister—and he had some time and wanted to see Utah."

"He's more than welcome and I think he'll be comfortable in the suite we gave him," she said, watching him bring a cup of freshly brewed coffee to the island and settle on a bar stool in front of her.

A memory of George sitting at her old kitchen island flashed in her head, but she tucked it away, refusing to go there.

Reaching over the space that separated them, he put a hand on hers. "You sure you're okay with this, MJ? I know it's...unconventional. I mean, me being gone a year and all."

"You explained it in your letter," she said. "And you certainly were generous with us."

He waved off the gratitude. "You and Cindy—everyone, really—thanked me enough last night. The fact is, I did what I set out to do. I gave just about everything away, but kept enough for me to live well, but not crazy. I won't have to fix toilets as a plumber, but I won't be flying on private planes, either."

She looked hard at him, the memories of her long and fun talks with this man flooding back. She'd deeply enjoyed their time together—more than a month of daily conversations, dinners, and enough time to really fall for each other.

When it ended rather abruptly, she'd realized how

familiar he'd become. She knew the silver threads in his hair, the strong shape of his nose, the hint of his upper lip under a surprisingly attractive moustache. She understood what made him tick and what his life had been like —she just hadn't known he was an extremely wealthy man.

"Now that I know what you were hiding," she said slowly, "I can tell that you were never comfortable with that wealth."

"I wasn't." He pulled back the cuff of a cable-knit sweater. "Look, Ma, no more Rolex."

She smiled. "So what are your plans, Matt? Are you staying through the holiday or..."

Inching back, he gave her a look of disbelief. "I, uh, thought I'd stay...as long as you'll have me."

What did that mean? She took a slow breath, holding his gaze. "I...I...would like—"

He held up a hand to stop her stammering. "I will not take a room or cabin indefinitely, I promise."

She laughed. "That's not..." She didn't know how to finish that.

"You do want me around, right?" he asked.

She lowered her wooden spoon, vaguely aware she hadn't done one thing to make a single pancake yet.

"Well, you're a distraction," she joked, trying to make light of all the emotions and uncertainty ricocheting through her.

"I don't want to confuse you," he said, flicking his thumb and index finger over his moustache as he sometimes did when he was struggling with how to say something important. "But I would like to...be with you."

She swallowed, feeling some blood drain from her face. *Be* with her? What did that mean, exactly?

"Starting with today," he said. "I have an idea. Are you busy?"

"Well..." Was she? "We still have friends in town and we'll be getting ready for a soft opening, so..."

"MJ." He slid off the stool and came around the counter, holding her gaze as he approached. "I didn't come to totally upset your apple cart."

She smiled. "You didn't?"

"Well, maybe tip it a little, but I feel like you're distant this morning. Are you *sure* you're okay with me being here?"

She had been far more than "okay" until that dang dream and the song and...George. Had he been sending her a message? Or was her imagination in overdrive?

"I love that you're here," she said, wanting to be fully honest. "It's...a lot. But I'm very, very happy you came back, Matt. I'm happy you're so interested in Park City."

He smiled, taking both her hands. "I am interested in Park City, along with a certain someone who lives here. In fact..." He made a face as though he didn't expect her to like what he was about to say. "That's what I wanted to do today."

"Tour the town?" she guessed, knowing he'd been everywhere last year.

"Tour an...open house. It's Sunday and there are a lot of them."

An open house? She just stared at him.

"I have to live somewhere," he said. "And...you're here, so..."

"You're moving here." It was a statement, but her voice cracked with surprise.

He didn't say anything, but there was a glimmer of disappointment in his eyes, and she hated that she'd put it there.

"Not if I'm not welcome.'"

"Matt!" She gripped his hands. "You're more than welcome. It's just..."

"I know, I know. Let's take it slow. I'll stay as a guest at Snowberry for the holiday season. I can do that, right?"

"Of course! We love having you *and* your nephew. It's perfect timing before we go into the high ski season."

"Then we'll slowly pick up where we left off. No big...changes. Just continue to get to know each other and see how that goes." He eased her closer. "But you need to know I've really missed you, Mary Jane."

She managed a shaky breath. "I really missed you, too, Graham Matthew."

He chuckled and gave her a light kiss on the forehead. "Dinner this week?"

"Of course."

"Maybe a sleigh ride, a trip to town, and you'll let me help you make my favorite scones."

She nodded. "Absolutely."

"Okay. I'm going to peek at those houses alone or with Wade, though. I do love it here and I sold my house in Florida."

"Give me a few days and I'll go with you," she said, letting him wrap her in a hug. "I'm still getting used to all of this."

He agreed, gave her a light kiss, and left to go back to his suite upstairs.

She took a minute to let it all sink in, then walked to her spacious pantry to get her pancakes started, a few more threads of confusion wrapping around her heart.

Maybe that's all the message from George really was —a warning call to not get swept up into something too fast or too serious. If that was the case, her late husband was, as usual, absolutely right.

Chapter Two
Gracie

"**P**oor Olivia," Benny said, shifting in his seat behind Gracie as she navigated the road that might have seen a snow plow this morning. Or maybe not, judging by the occasional whine of her bakery van tires.

"Poor? Not in this neighborhood," Gracie joked, getting glimpses of some of Park City's nicest real estate in the upscale and gated community that Marshall Hampton and his daughter, Olivia, called home.

"But she has to go to Los Angeles for Christmas!" Benny shook his head, cuddling Newt, his Cavapoo, closer for comfort. "I feel bad for her. And, trust me, she's not happy." On the next turn, he balanced the big Christmas bag with exploding tissue on the seat next to him. "I wonder if she'll be allowed to pack this science experiment kit in her suitcase so she has something to do."

Gracie laughed softly. "I'm sure her mom has plenty planned for her to do—there's a beach in L.A., you know, and...stars."

"Well, yes, there is an incredible observatory called Griffith. She'll definitely go there, since all she wants to do is be an astronaut. But, still, it's a horrible fate."

"Going to see her mom?" Gracie asked, not following. With one glance in the rearview mirror, she knew the fate was horrible for him, not Olivia. Benny and his best pal would certainly miss their time together, but...did that mean Gracie wouldn't see Olivia's father over the holidays?

She hoped not.

No surprise, her thoughts slipped back to Marshall Hampton, the man she was...could they call it dating? They'd made a gingerbread house together, they'd kissed—a decent amount—and he'd been her plus-one at Aunt Cindy's wedding two days ago.

They texted like teenagers, couldn't stop smiling when they were together, and had already talked about the possibility of combining their competing bakery businesses in Park City.

Yes, this was...something. She could not wait to find out what.

The house appeared between aspens—modern but warm, all stone and timber nestled into the hillside. Big windows caught the noon light like silver mirrors, the whole vibe perfectly understated but wealthy, just like the former NFL running back who owned the home.

Gracie had dropped Benny off here before, but only exchanged quick hellos and goodbyes from the driveway. Today, she felt invited and welcome, and her heart had been fluttering since breakfast even though they were just there to drop off Olivia's Christmas present.

Olivia opened a front door that was three times her size with a huge smile and an excited wave.

Behind her, a brindle border collie—the dog named Kat—trotted out, probably sensing her buddy Newt was in the car.

Olivia's espresso braids had recently been redone, falling in lovely cascades over her narrow shoulders, the style accentuating her big brown eyes. She looked like a mini version of her father right there, with rich dark skin and more confidence than Gracie could imagine having at eleven. At *any* age.

"Benny!" she called, prancing onto the spacious front porch in snowflake Christmas socks. "We got fresh snow! We can finally have our epic battle!"

"Do we have time, Mom?" Benny asked, clutching the bag and letting Newt run free up the stairs.

"We have a little bit of time before I have to get to work," she said, "and these guys have to go to the airport."

"It's fine," Olivia said, gathering Newt in her arms. "My dad said he wanted to talk to you about something, Miss Gracie."

He did? Gracie hoped that "something" was another date. And maybe it would involve another few kisses because...

She closed her eyes and let out a soft sigh. All she wanted to do was kiss that man.

She hung back a few seconds, taking a deep and steadying breath while the dogs barked, circled, and sniffed, then climbed the stairs.

"Are you excited about a trip to California, Olivia?"

The little girl froze, crossed her eyes, stuck out her tongue, and fisted her hands next to her face to show nothing but total disgust. Then it all disappeared into a sweet smile.

"I can't wait!" she exclaimed with undeniable eleven-year-old sarcasm.

"You'll go to the observatory, of course," Benny said, sarcasm missed. "I mean, I would on the first day."

"The observatory?" she scoffed. "Have you met my mom? No, of course you haven't. The only thing she observes is herself. I'm sure we'll hit Rodeo Drive, though."

"It's pronounced *ro*-dee-o, Olivia, not ro-*day*-o," Benny corrected, looking a little smug because one-upping his fellow genius and best friend was a rare opportunity, indeed.

She looked at Gracie and executed yet another eyeroll. "Gotcha. Come on in."

Before Gracie took another step, Marshall appeared behind his daughter, one arm braced against the doorframe. He looked maddeningly relaxed in a soft gray sweater and jeans, his eyes easy and warm as he looked at Gracie.

There was just a hint of invitation in their dark depths, enough to keep her pulse a few beats too fast.

"Welcome to Chez Hampton," he joked, waving Benny in and reaching for Gracie's hand. "Not one word about the lack of a Christmas tree, please."

"You don't have a tree?" Benny stopped mid-step, looking up. "It's after Thanksgiving."

Olivia laughed. "What can I say? He's a rule-follower, Dad."

"I like that about you, Ben." He gave Benny a high-five, and then a secret, sexy wink to Gracie that darn near melted her on the front stairs. He always called him "Ben," which Gracie knew her son loved because it made him feel like Marshall's peer.

Inside, she stepped out of her wet boots and glanced around the formal entryway—hardwood floors, an Oriental rug that probably cost more than her car, and no place for boots.

"We never use this door," Marshall said, seeing her dilemma as he lifted her boots from the floor. "Come to the kitchen where it's warm and there's coffee, tea, and a mudroom."

"Also, Dad made almond flour monk fruit biscotti," Olivia finished, leaning into Gracie. "I know how you *love* a sugar-free treat, Miss Gracie."

Gracie just laughed and glanced into a glorious living room that somehow managed to be masculine and perfectly decorated.

Maybe a little too perfectly—definitely what she'd call "model home" flawless, with a floor plan that took advantage of a sweeping view of the snow-streaked mountain peaks and some ski lifts in the distance.

She checked it out while Marshall made small talk with Benny, and they all ended up in an enormous contemporary kitchen. There, more sunshine streamed over marble counters and pale oak cabinets.

Olivia bounced on her toes. "Benny! The snow is perfect and I'm going to stupid sunny Calif—"

"Liv." Marshall gave a quick warning look. "It's not stupid."

"Well, I don't know why Mom had to move there. If she was still in Pittsburgh, at least I could see my old friends. But, no, she had to go to California." Olivia sighed dramatically, lifting a jacket from a hook in the mudroom off the kitchen where Gracie hung hers.

Gracie knew enough about Marshall's shared custody arrangement to understand that he'd had Olivia last year for Christmas, so this holiday was for Bianca.

"How much time do I have left, Dad?" Olivia asked.

Marshall glanced at his watch. "Your mother lands in a few hours. She has to deplane, meet us outside of security, then get you back to the gate for the flight back to L.A. So, we have to leave here at one o'clock at the latest."

"And I need to get to work, Benny," Gracie said. "We should let the kids exchange gifts and get out of your hair."

"My hair needs snow in it!" Olivia announced, grabbing Benny's arm to yank him through the mudroom and back into his boots. "We have time for me to destroy you in a snowball fight. Can we take the dogs?"

"Until they get cold," Marshall said, laughing at his whirlwind of a daughter.

Benny grinned. "You're going down, Olivia."

"Am not!"

Kids and dogs disappeared outside, and almost immediately, Gracie spotted them running off a snow-covered deck into the yard.

"I thought they'd do science experiments," she said, laughing. "Instead, war."

Marshall leaned closer, voice low. "War will keep them occupied." He slipped his arm around her waist and pulled her into him. "And we'll have...peace."

He punctuated that with the lightest kiss, holding her against his broad chest, his strong athlete's arm lifting her an inch off the floor with ease.

When she came back to Earth, breathing was...a challenge.

"So this wasn't all just a dream," she whispered.

He smiled and kissed her forehead. "It's a dream, all right." He looked down at her, nothing but warmth and kindness and goodness in his ebony eyes. "Can I get you something? Coffee or tea? Sugarless biscotti?"

"Tea would be great." Somehow, she managed to ease away, nodding. "If it's got peppermint and not... peptides."

He groaned and punched his chest. "And she mocks."

"Playfully," she assured him, slipping onto a barstool at an island the size of, well, a football field.

He poured steaming water into two mugs while she watched the kids play, flashes of color and movement against the snow.

"Olivia's going to be a mess before her flight," she mused.

"I think that's her evil plan." He brought the mugs over. "Make her mother mad."

"Do they not get along?" she asked.

He shrugged. "Bianca's not maternal and Olivia is...a unique challenge."

She shifted her gaze to catch that unique challenge clocking Benny with a snow explosion, making him collapse in laughter.

"I love her," she whispered, barely aware of the confession. Then she faced him, expecting to blush, but for some reason her body cooperated. "She's brought such a light to Benny's life."

He smiled behind his mug, taking a sip as he sat next to her. "That goes both ways, believe me."

Gracie cradled the mug. "So, what's on your mind? Olivia said you wanted to talk about something. Is it about...combining our businesses?" They'd talked about that idea a few times, both of them feeling the sting of having a competing bakery across the street from one another.

Their "brands" were quite different, but they'd been toying with the idea of combining her decadent desserts and his healthy options to improve both bottom lines.

"Sort of," he said, the words sounding oddly cryptic.

"Well, I've been thinking about it, Marshall, and I do believe there's a way we could save rental money and offer Park City the best of Craving Clean and Sugarfall."

He eyed her, amusement flickering in his expression. "You do, huh?"

"I do," she said, trying to interpret the way he asked the question. "Don't you? Or have you changed your mind about some kind of merger?"

"Some kind," he said.

She took a sip, waited, then asked, "What are you, um, thinking? Looking for a new place completely or just taking over the space next to mine or even folding Craving Clean into Sugarfall? Selling each other's products? I can—"

"I'm not thinking about any of those logistics, Gracie."

She lowered the cup. "So you did change your mind."

"I did not," he assured her. "But I'm thinking about... a different kind of...combined effort." He sighed and laughed softly. "I don't want to get all wrapped up in semantics and lose the point of what's on my mind."

Studying him, she frowned, definitely lost. "What's on your mind?"

"You."

The single, simple syllable hit hard. "Oh," she breathed her response. "That's...unexpected."

"Is it?" he asked, leaning closer. "You kissed me goodbye after the wedding like it was very...expected."

She felt her signature blush rise to the surface. "It was an unexpectedly nice kiss," she whispered, letting the play on words cover the fact that much more of this banter and there would be another unexpectedly nice kiss.

He exhaled again, pressing his hands on the counter as though he had to steady himself for the conversation.

"Marshall? Is everything okay?"

"Yes," he said slowly. "I hope it will be after...this."

A shiver danced up her spine at the way he said it. "After what?"

"Well, Olivia is leaving," he started.

"And Benny's sad about that," she said. "I'm sure you are, too."

"I am, but...it really frees me up. And that's what I wanted to talk to you about."

"Oh?"

He turned to face her, reaching for her to do the same. "Not about work, but about...life. Our lives. Together. As a couple."

More shivers exploded on her arms. "A couple?" Her heart did a little dance. "That sounds...nice."

"But there are some things you should know about me," he said softly. "So, if I can be brutally honest and you don't go running out into the snow like your hair's on fire..."

And then the dancing stopped and her heart fell. What was he about to confess? She took a deep breath and looked right at him, ready for anything. Almost anything.

"I won't run," she assured him. "And I appreciate honesty."

"Good, 'cause I'm coming at you with a boatload of it."

She swallowed, and waited.

"I don't date..." he began.

Okay, well, that wasn't good.

"*Casually,*" he finished, emphasizing the word. "I

never have, to be real with you. It's something my mother sort of pounded into me."

She thought of some of the endearing stories he'd told her about his hardworking, Jesus-loving mother, Germaine.

"My mom taught me not to...I think the word she liked to use was 'window-shop' with women," he told her.

Window-shop?

He took her hand in his. "'What's the use,' Mom would say. 'Don't pluck things off the shelf and try them on for fun, Marshall.'" He used a slightly higher-pitched voice and a playful accent to imitate her.

But Gracie didn't laugh because...what exactly was he saying?

"So I don't," he finished. "I don't date around or look for the next relationship or play the field—unless it's a gridiron and the QB just handed me the ball." He grinned. "Once I see what I want, I...make it mine or I don't." One heartbeat, then two passed while he held her gaze. "Can you tell where I'm going with this?"

She could hope, but she wasn't sure. "Maybe. Keep going."

"Okay, well, when I look at you, I see...a future."

She just stared at him, her pulse racing so hard she could barely hear him as he made his sweet speech, making her sock-covered toes curl around the footrest of the bar stool.

"Too much? Too soon?" he asked, squeezing her hand. "I just have to be honest."

"No, no, it's fine." She almost laughed at the understatement. Fine? It was...*glorious.*

"And, assuming—hoping, actually—that you feel the same way," he continued, "I'd like to spend the next few weeks right next to you."

"I'd...like that," she managed to say.

"I mean, I know you have Benny and a family and a business," he added. "And things are busy this time of year. But I'd like to quite intentionally take time for us. I want to go out to dinner, and spend some full days together, put up my tree together, and take long rides into the mountains, and just sink into this relationship and see if I'm...right."

"Right?" she echoed, still stuck imagining the canvas of romance he'd just painted for her.

"Gracie, I think this—us, we—have something special." His thumb brushed her knuckles, steady and sure when she felt anything but. "I don't want to rush you or scare you, but I don't want to take two years of dating to get where I really hope we're going."

Her chest squeezed as she let out a soft laugh. "Well, it's not that rushed, considering I've had a crush on you the size of a mountain since the day we met a year ago."

A slow smile lit his whole face. "You have? Me, too! Like...I feel like I've been climbing Mount Crushmore."

She threw her head back and laughed at that, relief and joy surging through her. "Really? I had no idea!"

"Are you kidding? Did you notice how we always seemed to bump into each other on the street in front of our shops...*by chance?*"

"Not by chance?" she guessed.

"I watch the front door of Sugarfall like the prover-bial hawk and the minute I see you step out, I need air. Well, I need...Gracie. I didn't think you'd be interested, since I was competing for your business. Then we made that gingerbread house, and then the night of the ice skating..."

"You weren't sure you could trust me," she reminded him.

"A big fat excuse for how hard and fast I was falling."

"Aw, Marshall." She blinked, a little embarrassed that the words made her tear up.

"Then after the wedding, when we kissed..." He inched closer. "I really hoped I had a shot."

A shot? Was he crazy? "And you couldn't tell by how much I stammer and blush and try to look anywhere but at you because..." She bit her lip. "Never mind."

He leaned in and kissed her. "Not never mind. This is what I want to talk about. You, me, our kids, our lives, our hopes and dreams and past and...future." Another kiss. "Because I think there can be one, Gracie, and I'm just warning you. I was famous for how fast I was on the football field. Speed made my career. And when it comes to love, I plan to be the same way."

Did he say *love*?

Taking a deep breath, she put a hand on his arm, taking hold of a mighty shoulder she ached to lean on for...for a long, long time.

"Then my answer is yes, Marshall. Let's spend all the time we can together and see where it takes us."

He answered with another kiss, longer this time, the connection warm and sweet. She let herself sink deeply into the delicious moment, stunned by how much she wanted love and a future and a man who was honest, kind, and present.

She'd done such a good job at denial that—

The doorbell rang, pulling them apart.

"That's Amazon," he said, standing with a regretful smile. "Olivia put in an overnight order for a Christmas present for her mom, since she totally forgot. Do not move, Gracie McBride. I'll be right back."

"Go save the holiday. I'll just be here...floating."

With one more light kiss, he disappeared down the hall.

She stayed where she was, touching her lips, basking in that dizzy, sweet glow. He felt that way about her? He wanted to spend the holiday together talking about...the future?

This just officially became the very best Christmas ever in all her thirty-six years of life on Earth. Nothing could compare to what he'd just laid out for the next few weeks.

Through the window, Benny and Olivia flung snowballs with wild precision, their laughter ringing clear. The dogs were done, though, shivering on the top stair.

Gracie stood to let them in, not surprised her legs were like jelly when she tried to walk.

"Merry Christmas, darling!" The woman's voice rang out from the front of the house, rich and unmistakably confident.

"Bianca? What are you doing here?"

What? Bianca was here—*now?* Well, at least he didn't have to drive to the airport. And Gracie got to meet her, which was probably a good thing.

"Change of plans!" the woman announced, bright as the sun outside. "I'm spending the holiday here with you. Like a family. Can you get those bags from the Uber driver, Marsh? So much better for Olivia, don't you think?"

Gracie froze in the mudroom, her hand on the knob to the patio door.

Silence stretched, then Marshall's low, uneasy murmur. "No, no," he said. "That's not a good idea, Bianca..."

Oh, boy. They needed to talk—alone. Gracie grabbed her jacket from the hook and stuffed her feet into her boots in one lightning move, ready to vanish into the backyard and let him handle it privately.

But as she opened the door at the back of the mudroom, Newt came bounding in, followed by Kat, both dogs panting, covered in snow.

"Whoa, whoa, hold on there, kids," she called, snagging their collars, knowing they'd go for the stranger who'd just blown in to wreck the dreamiest Christmas Gracie could imagine.

"Where's my little Olivia?" the woman called, voice and heels getting louder and closer.

Still struggling to hold the dogs, Gracie glanced up just as the other woman walked into the kitchen.

In that instant, Gracie looked into the lion's gold eyes

of the single most beautiful creature she'd ever seen. Statuesque, with sleek black hair and creamed-coffee skin and dramatically made-up eyes, Bianca Hampton radiated confidence and attitude and very expensive perfume.

"Oh!" Bianca's eyes flicked over Gracie. "Hello. I heard you got a dog, Marsh. Two? Then it was smart to get a dog walker. Where is Olivia? I can't wait to tell her I'm staying until the New Year!"

The New Year? A dog walker?

For a split second, Gracie considered letting go of the collars, knowing that winter white wool coat would suffer the brunt of the decision.

Instead, she held tight, straightened, and looked directly at Bianca. "I'll get her."

Pulling the slightly unwilling dogs with her, she pushed open the door with her hip and stepped out onto the patio just as the biggest, fastest, coldest snowball in history hit her square in the face.

"Mom! Oh, no! I'm so sorry! Mom! I didn't mean to…"

Benny's wail faded away as Gracie blinked into the snowflakes.

Life, not Benny's wayward snowball, had just smacked her hard in the face.

🌲

GRACIE WIPED snow from her lashes with the back of her hand, blinking while Benny gave her a crumpled tissue he dug out of his pocket.

"I'm fine," she said, laughing like that might make it true.

Newt pressed his warm little body to her shin, contrite as if this was all his fault, while Kat hovered nearby, uncertain which human needed comforting more.

"Mom, I'm so sorry," Benny whined again.

Olivia came tearing over. "Miss Gracie, are you—"

"Your mother's here," she said, trying to make her voice sound bright but the words still came out like a death sentence.

"Mom? Here? In this house?" Olivia stepped by her toward the door, snagging Kat on the way. "What the heck?"

She disappeared inside while Gracie stood frozen—almost literally, but definitely in her heart—with Benny.

"Why is she here?" Benny asked. "I thought Olivia was meeting her at the airport."

Gracie closed her eyes and tried to hold it together. "I guess she changed plans. I don't know. Come on, let's get you and Newt inside. It's cold."

They stepped into the mudroom and voices carried from the kitchen—Bianca's lilting and self-assured, followed by Marshall's low and careful responses. Olivia was uncharacteristically quiet.

After they took off their boots and jackets and

brushed off Newt, Gracie and Benny stepped around the corner into the kitchen.

"So this in Benny!" Bianca cooed, coming over to him with arms out. "My Liv talks endlessly about you." She hugged him tight and he stood, awkward, in a stranger's arms. "And you're Benny's mom," she added, pinning Gracie with a shockingly direct and impossibly perfect gaze. "I'm sorry I mistook you for the dog walker. You're her friend's mother."

That was one way of describing her.

"Gracie McBride." Gracie took a few steps forward, hand extended. "Welcome to Park City. First time?"

"Not really." She sent a coy look at one very uncomfortable Marshall, who braced himself on the countertop as though Hurricane Bianca could wipe them all out.

Well, she'd certainly done a number on his big Christmas plans.

"Remember, we were here with your coach and his wife," she cooed at Marshall. "We stayed in that astounding three-story Airbnb and skied for days. Oh, I loved it. In fact, it was that trip that made me call the airlines and get on an earlier flight so I could surprise you. I brought all my ski gear."

She turned to Olivia and flashed a smile that was white and perfect and, yes, genuine as she gazed at her daughter.

Of course she loved Olivia. Marshall had said that Bianca was not "maternal" but who didn't truly love their daughter? She wasn't the enemy—just the ex.

"And look at you, Liv." She opened her arms. Olivia

hesitated—just a flicker—then hugged her mother. "It's been too long, right?"

Marshall had shared that his ex had moved to L.A. in search of fame and fortune, always having excuses for why she didn't see Olivia. But no excuse now, it seemed.

"Isn't it good news?" Bianca asked. "You don't have to get on a plane today."

Olivia pulled back. "We're not leaving at all?" She sounded hopeful and surprised and maybe a little worried.

"Why would we?" Bianca trilled a laugh and glanced at Marshall, her gaze just as warm. "Christmas is about family, so we're going to spend the holiday here." She hugged Olivia harder, eyes still on her ex-husband. "Because we Hamptons are a *family*."

She stressed the word as though it needed extra emphasis.

Olivia frowned, clearly weighing the news in her sharp and analytical brain. "So... I don't have to leave Park City?"

"No, you don't," Bianca said, smoothing her daughter's sleeve. "Isn't that wonderful? We'll do Christmas in Park City! We can hit the slopes, shop in town, go out to dinner. It'll be such fun, right, Marsh?"

He swallowed. "Where are you staying?"

"Oh, well..." She huffed a frustrated breath. "My decision was so last-minute, I'm still scrambling for an Airbnb or something. Goodness, though, this town is crowded with tourists over the holidays. The decent places are booked through New Year's. Lifts are open, and there's a waiting list everywhere. I guess I could just drag her to some motel on the highway."

She waited a beat, looking at him with an expectant expression.

"Or..." She pressed her hands into a praying pose against her lips, all but batting her lash extensions at her ex-husband. "This place looks big. I'm sure you have a guest wing or—"

"That's not going to work," he replied, leaving no room for argument.

"Oh..." She pouted. "That's a shame, Marsh. I won't be any trouble, I swear. I don't eat much, I sleep late, and Olivia and I are supposed to be together this holiday."

"But you and I aren't," he said.

"Oh, Marsh. It's Christmas!"

Gracie took a step back, everything introverted in her really wanting to hide while Marshall and Bianca hashed this out.

"And this is my house at Christmas," he said. "Of course you should spend your Christmas with Olivia any way you like. But not...here. Not in this house."

"Oh, dear. I guess this was a bad idea," Bianca said.

Marshall gave a soft "ya think" snort, but Olivia stepped up, looking...yeah, hopeful. She wanted her mom to stay here.

"I could still be with both of you that way, Dad," she said. "I mean, Mom and I would do things but we could..." Her voice faded as Marshall looked at her, the war of emotions evident on his face.

He wanted Bianca to leave. He wanted Olivia to be

happy. And as of ten minutes ago, he wanted a future with Gracie.

A beat passed and everyone in the room looked at Marshall, who had just enough pain in his eyes for Gracie to feel it.

He shouldn't have to justify not hosting his ex. He also shouldn't be the villain in Olivia's eyes. And Bianca had a point about the timing—Park City was packed.

Gracie cleared her throat, already knowing exactly what to say even before she opened her mouth. It was the right thing to do—not ideal, but right.

"Actually," she said, and four faces turned. "There's another option. My family happens to own a lodge with plenty of beautiful cabins available this month. We just finished renovations and haven't officially opened, so..."

"Miss Gracie!" Olivia exclaimed. "That's perfect! And Mom, I can stay with you!"

"We can have more epic snowball battles," Benny chimed in after staying weirdly silent all this time.

"And take sleigh rides and go sledding and it's really close to the ski resort and, Mom, you'll love Snowberry Lodge!" Olivia was practically jumping with excitement, but Bianca did not look happy.

"Snowberry..." She cringed. "That sounds...quaint."

"It is," Gracie said. "My mother and aunt are having a soft opening of the newly renovated cabins this week. You could have the one that has two bedrooms and a fantastic mountain view."

Bianca didn't look convinced. "Is it...nice? I'm not a

snob, but I like my Egyptian cotton sheets and room service."

"It's lovely," Gracie replied, confident that was the truth. "Everything's new and fresh, and I don't know about room service, but my mom runs the kitchen and she'll make you anything you'd like, any hour you'd like it."

"Your...mom." She practically groaned and glanced at Marshall as if he had to know that family-owned mountain lodges were not her thing.

But he visibly brightened. "It's a solution," he said. "You'll be comfortable and you'd be..."

Not here, Gracie imagined him thinking.

"Close," he finished.

"This is so cool," Benny exclaimed, scooping up Newt for a furry kiss. "The dogs can run around Snowberry."

"We can hang out all the time, Benny!"

"And maybe, if you ever open that present, do a science experiment."

"Is that what you gave me?" she asked, her eyes shining. "I'm dead. My gift's the same thing!"

"No way! I don't believe you."

"Come and see it!"

Giggling, they high-fived and took off toward the den together, their little problems solved.

Bianca moaned. "This is not what I had in mind," she said under her breath to Marshall, almost as if she didn't realize—or care—that Gracie was still standing there.

"Really, I'd hoped I could stay here and we could...reconnect, Marsh."

Oh, boy. Gracie braced for him to relent, to take one long look at that shockingly beautiful woman—her skin didn't even look real, it was so luscious—and realize he shouldn't have let her go.

But he just closed his eyes and shook his head. "I'm pretty busy over the holidays."

She inched back at the tone, then turned. "Then thank goodness you happen to be here, Gretchen."

"Gracie," she corrected.

"Of course. I'm sorry. This is very kind of you. Thank you."

"I can drive you," Gracie suggested, before Bianca the Beautiful did a full-court press and Marshall caved. "We can be there in ten minutes, fifteen if the plows are running behind."

Bianca sighed in defeat. "Please tell me there's a decent espresso between here and there."

"Three," Marshall said, fighting a smile that made Gracie wonder if he was amused by the woman—or totally over her. Gracie didn't know but she decided right then and there that she would not be jealous.

Sure, Bianca was drop-dead gorgeous and had just kicked a Christmas dream to the curb, but Gracie was not going to step one toe into jealousy. Bianca was the past and Marshall had said himself that Gracie could be the future. She'd cling to that with all she had.

"Olivia's bags are in the garage," Marshall said.

"Come with me, Gracie, and we'll transfer them to your van."

"And I'll take the self-guided tour," Bianca quipped, barely hiding the distaste in her voice as she walked off in the direction of the living room.

The minute they were through the mudroom and alone in the garage, Marshall turned to Gracie and took her hands. "Thank you and I'm sorry. I'd drive her there myself, but she makes my head explode."

"It's fine. She's quite...something."

He rolled his eyes, looking so much like Olivia that Gracie had to laugh. "The list is long of the somethings she is," he cracked. "But you, sweet Gracie, saved this from getting messy and me from having to get a motel because she moved in here."

"I could feel it all going sideways," she admitted.

"Oh, it fell on its backside," he grumbled. Then he leaned closer. "This does not change a thing that we just talked about." At her look, he chuckled. "Okay, it's a small change. But I meant what I said, Gracie. I still want this time and this holiday with you. Only you. Olivia has to be with her—by agreement and by law."

"I understand," she assured him. "Just...tell me when."

"Tonight?" He pulled her closer, stealing the briefest kiss—sweet and quick. "Don't say no."

"Gracie?" The mudroom door popped open. "Ready when you are?"

"Just meet us out front, Bianca," Marshall said. Then,

when she was gone, he gave Gracie an expectant look. "I have to go into Craving Clean later. You're working?"

"I can be done around four," she said. "My night manager can close."

"Perfect. I'll get you then. We can walk around town, have an early dinner, and come back here to decorate my tree. I'll bring it down from the attic while you get Bianca and Olivia to the lodge. Sound like a plan?"

"It's a..."

"A date," he finished, stealing one more kiss. "First of many."

She sure hoped so.

Chapter Three

Copper's hooves made that steady, soothing crunch that Elise Hale loved to hear the most. The sound of this horse's steps across the hay of Snowberry's stable, headed to the paddock with Elise on his back, was music to her ears.

The horse's flaxen mane fluttered against a rich reddish brown coat, while his warm breaths puffed clouds into the crisp mountain air. Elise sat tall in the saddle, confident in how her body fit in the curved leather and secure harness that would keep her from falling if she suddenly started to slide to one side or the other.

Her gloved hands kept a loose grip on the reins as she grinned down at her friend and future sister-in-law. Of course, Nicole was beaming. Every time she got Elise on this horse, Nicole was happy.

And so was Elise. The only way it could be better would be to get on this horse alone and ride without an escort. But that was never to be, so she basked content-edly in what she had—some freedom and access to a horse.

In fact, there were few places on Earth where Elise

felt more content and at home than on this horse. Maybe in the teaching barn at the Great Basin Veterinary Institute, where she was starting her second year of graduate school. Or around the dinner table with her family—that was always a happy place.

But riding Copper—a thrill that Nicole had made possible last Christmas and continued all through the year—was definitely her greatest joy.

"Can you believe it's been a whole year?" Elise asked as she thought about it. "I still remember the first time you—and your dad, Red, and Cam—got me up on this king and my life changed."

Nicole looked up at her, dark eyes dancing as she no doubt remembered how they'd dragged the rig and rolled Elise to her first taste of heaven in fourteen long years. Before the car accident that put her in a wheelchair, Elise had been a superstar competitive rider.

"Your life changed in more ways than one," Nicole said. "That was the day you told me about your dreams to be a vet."

Another thing that wouldn't have happened without Nicole Kessler, who'd risked her romance with Cameron to push for Elise's independence.

"And you made those dreams come true." Elise sighed, awash with affection and appreciation. So much so that she had to fight the urge to put a hand on Nicole's shoulder, but she never let go of the western saddle's horn with her non-rein hand.

A paraplegic couldn't be too careful. The seat may have become as comfortable as her normal ride, and under it she had a secure but invisible harness, but one slip could be a lot more dangerous than falling from her wheelchair.

"You're the one making your dreams come true, E," Nicole replied, using the simple nickname that Elise's brother had hung on her when she was about three. "You're absolutely killing it at Great Basin, not that I'm surprised."

"Oh, speaking of school, I forgot to tell you I accepted the ultimate extra-curricular challenge. They have a hard time finding volunteers for the Live Nativity at the institute because it's between semesters. So...yours truly was selected—and by that, I mean no one else volunteered—as the program manager this year."

"Really? A Live Nativity? Like with real animals?"

"Well, we are a veterinary school. It's on Christmas Eve, right on the campus quad. Real people playing Mary, Joseph, and baby J, and—the big draw at GBVI—actual sheep, a donkey, and one particularly dramatic goat who thinks he's an understudy for Jesus and tries to get in the manger. Wise men, too, but no camels."

"I bet kids love that," Nicole said as they stepped through the wide barn doors to the paddock that Elise would circle on Copper for as long as she could. "We'll have to make a family outing and take Benny. Are you in it?"

She snorted. "No wheelchairs in Bethlehem at the time. My job is to coordinate actors, the set, costumes, and props—which is mostly done by email and a few meetings—and to supervise the care of the animals."

"That sounds like a big job."

"It's manageable. Since the event takes place after the semester has ended, a lot of the faculty and students are gone, so...they scraped the bottom of the barrel and got 'Hale on Wheels.'"

Nicole cracked up at the nickname Elise's classmates had given her. "I'm so glad you have friends and a rich life, E."

Did she have a rich life, Elise wondered as she sat tall and proud on Copper while Nicole opened the paddock gate. She certainly had a fine circle of friends, a true purpose, and a bright future as a vet.

The year of independence at the school a little more than an hour away had done wonders for Elise. She was still careful—still cautious about getting stuck or stranded—but she was finally living the wheelchair version of a life she'd only dreamed about before.

She didn't have *everything*, but she had a lot. And what she didn't have, she didn't obsess over.

Copper flicked an ear, and she rubbed his neck. "He's walking easier today. I'm glad that joint supplement I recommended helped."

"Thank you, Dr. Hale on Wheels. Please tell me that's going to be the name of your vet practice."

"It might be," Elise said, lifting her gaze to scan the sunbathed paddock, checking out the small snowdrifts and...whoa...*cowboy.*

"Who is *that?*"

Nicole angled her head and peered through

sunglasses in the direction of Elise's locked gaze. "Oh, that's Wade Reynolds."

"Guest at the lodge?"

"Yes and no," Nicole said. "He's Matt Walker's nephew."

"Oh, the lottery man courting Aunt MJ," Elise said, completely up to speed on the latest gossip at Snowberry. "His nephew, huh?" She eyed the tall man who wore a soft down vest over a plaid flannel shirt, and a cowboy hat that screamed country songs about whiskey and women and well-loved trucks.

Sauntering down the road from the cabins to the lodge, he paused at the paddock when he saw Copper. He leaned against the wood, one boot hooked on the bottom rail, his gloved hands resting on the top as he watched.

"Did he come to check out Aunt MJ and make sure she's not trying to siphon millions from his rich Uncle Matt?" Elise asked.

Nicole chuckled. "Girl, you watch too much Lifetime TV. Also, he calls Matt Graham, which is slightly confusing, but remember, Matt used his middle name to hide his millions."

"And you say *I* watch too much Lifetime?"

"True. Anyway, apparently Wade has never been to Utah and came along with his uncle. He hasn't been around much, but I've said hello."

"He's cute. I mean, if you like sexy cowboys with square jaws and a day's worth of whiskers and jeans that fit like...like, holy moly, there should be laws against that. I ask you—*who* likes that?"

Nicole snorted. "Not me, but I'm about to marry your brother." She leaned close enough to press her shoulder into Copper's flank. "You, however, are quite single."

And paralyzed from the hips down. But Elise didn't say that because...right now, sitting on this horse and feeling like she owned the world, she *wasn't* paralyzed.

At least not to a stranger, not for five minutes. The fantasy of it was too irresistible. "Introduce me, Nic."

"Of course. You're in charge of the horse, so head on over."

She lifted the reins ever so slightly—Copper could read her every move now—and Hot Cowboy must have sensed their attention because he lifted his chin slightly, meeting Elise's gaze across the paddock.

For a second, she forgot to breathe. Then he smiled— slow, crooked, devastating.

Her pulse tripped. "Oh, boy."

Nicole laughed. "I'm going with man, not boy. All I know is he's about thirty and has a toe-curling Southern accent."

If only her toes *could* curl.

She kicked the thought away with imaginary toes that *did* work, and rode closer to the cowboy named Wade.

When they stopped a few feet away, he tipped his hat, revealing that it covered dark brown hair that looked like he'd tried to tame it and given up halfway through. His eyes were startling—a green so bright they almost looked lit from within.

"Mornin', ladies," he drawled. "Didn't mean to interrupt. Just admirin' the view."

Elise's lips curved before she could stop them. "I'll assume you mean the horse."

He chuckled, the sound low and warm. "Well, ma'am, I don't limit my admiration."

Elise arched a brow. "Smooth-talker. Also, I just got ma'amed."

"My mama raised me that way," he said easily. "It's the way we do things where I'm from in Alabama."

Elise's grin widened at the way he dragged out the state's name, emphasis on at least two syllables.

"Wade, this is Elise Hale," Nicole said, making the introduction easily, "who will be my sister-in-law in two-and-a-half weeks. Elise, meet Wade Reynolds, our guest from the Deep South."

"Welcome to Utah." She clutched the horn with her left hand and bravely reached out her right, certain that Wade didn't notice Nicole's subtle move to hold Elise's leg safely in the tiny harness that only a trained eye would see.

Smooth, Nic. I'll pay you in hundreds later.

"Thank you kindly," Wade said. "I admit, I've fallen in love."

Elise gave a saucy lift to her shoulder. "Already? We just met."

He laughed heartily, deep from inside his very impressive flannel-clad chest. "Doesn't take long when a woman's on a horse."

She patted Copper's mane, a thrill jolting through

her. Had she ever flirted with a man before? Sure, she was flirty by nature. But one who hadn't met her in a wheelchair? No, never. Not once in her adult life.

"I've fallen for the mountains, too," he clarified, taking a quick glance to the peaks against the blue sky, but then his gaze moved right back to Elise as if...well, as if she were even prettier than those mountains.

She was pretty—she'd always known that. And she took great care with her hair, makeup, and fashion because it was all she could control of her body.

But right this minute, under the winter sun, high on Copper's back, bantering with a gorgeous cowboy who thought she was as normal as the next girl? Honey, she could climb that Rocky Mountain high all day long.

"My uncle told me the lodge had a horse, and I'm partial to anything with four legs and an attitude. Figured I'd say hello."

"Copper's the sweetest guy alive," Elise told him. "A total teddy bear. Unless you're a peppermint candy, then you're just his next snack."

"Duly noted," he said. "You ride often?"

"Every chance I get."

Before she could answer, Red's booming voice cut through the air. "Nicole! Hey, I need you a minute!"

They all turned to see him on the far side of the paddock, tugging hard at an open Santa jacket. "Can you help before the sleigh ride passengers show up? This darn coat musta shrunk since last time I had it on."

"Oh, I'm sure that's what happened," Nicole cracked on a whisper. "No cream puffs involved. I'll be right back." She gave Elise a quick look, a secret question in her eyes. "Are you..."

"Go save Red." She let her eyes widen slightly, hoping her friend got the message that she'd be fine, she wouldn't fall, and she didn't want this moment to end.

"Be right back," she repeated, heading off across the paddock.

More hundreds for Nic. Many more.

It was a rare moment that Elise sat alone on a horse, and even more rare to be a foot above a *dime* who looked at her like she'd hung the moon with one hand and the stars with the other.

"I have to say..." Wade tipped his hat back far enough that it was about as secure on his head as Elise's behind in this saddle. "Everything about Utah is gorgeous, and I do mean *everything*."

Dude was a first-class, Grade A, woman-melting flirt. And she was so here for it.

"Thank you," she said, not even trying to pretend to be coy. "Do you ski?"

"I'm from Mobile, honey. That's like askin' one of you folks if you wrestle gators," he said with a laugh.

"Do *you* wrestle gators?" she asked.

"Only if they're sick and, in my case, have a tumor."

She managed to inch back, the serious word so out of character with the flirty guy. "A...tumor?"

"I'm a veterinary oncologist."

"No!" she said on a gasp. Instantly sensing the sound might send Nicole nearly flying over, she flicked her hand in that direction to stop her. "You're a vet?"

"I studied at Auburn and just finished residency. I have a few certifications to pass, then I'll be official. Hopefully"—he reached over the railing and patted Copper's head with a sure, confident hand—"this fella will never need to see me."

"Oncology?" For a moment, she forgot to be witty, taken by the information. "We don't have that department yet."

He cocked his head. "Well, this place is small and there's only one horse."

She laughed. "No, I meant at Great Basin Veterinary Institute. I'm starting my second year there."

It was his turn to look shocked. "You're in vet school?"

She nodded, unable to hide her pride. "The institute is outside of Salt Lake, in a town called Eagle Mountain."

"It sounds as beautiful as everything else in this state."

"It is," she agreed.

"I'd love to see it," he said, a slow smile pulling. "With the right tour guide, that is."

She started to smile, but an age-old burn in her stomach came back to life. For a flash, she'd been normal. Now, the truth would have to come out.

Nicole came jogging over, probably freaking out that she'd left Elise alone on Copper for so long. Cameron would flip out, but Elise didn't care.

"Everything good?" Nicole asked.

"Great," Elise said, too quickly.

"Elise is going to show me around her vet institute,"

Wade said with the confidence of a man who'd never gotten turned down by a woman in his life.

"You are?" Nicole's face brightened. "How fun."

Would it be fun? Or would it be miserable? Because watching his face fall when she rolled out of her ADA-approved campus apartment and revealed that she was Hale on Wheels was actually the stuff of misery.

"Well, I'm busy with the Live Nativity program—"

"Nothing like a Christmas display that actually smells like the real thing," he joked, making her laugh.

"Sounds like you've been to one."

"It's standard at every vet school," he said.

"You're a vet, too?" Nicole asked.

"Oncology," he said, with a tone that told Elise it was truly his greatest accomplishment and she so understood and adored that.

Please, God, don't make me like him any more than I already do.

"Well, I better not keep you from getting Copper warmed up for his sleigh ride," he said, even giving her a reason to continue riding in the paddock.

She'd never have to come clean. She could ride away into the stable and leave this intriguing man thinking she was...normal.

Sadly, she wasn't and never would be.

"I'll get your number from Nicole and we'll set up a visit," he said, then must have seen the look on her face, because he lowered his chin, the picture of humility. "If you like, that is."

Did she *like*? In one way, more than anything. In

another? All she wanted was to be someone else in a working body.

"Of course," she said, hearing a bit of her spunk fade with the words.

"I'll text you, Elise." Wade tipped his hat. "Nice meetin' you. See you soon."

With that, he strode away toward the lodge, six-foot-something and so gorgeous that all she could do was stare at his back and whimper.

"Well, well, well." Nicole clucked noisily enough to get Copper's attention. "Look who has a date."

"Stop!" The order sounded harsh, and Elise regretted it the minute she spoke.

"Why?"

She huffed out a breath, turning Copper to head back to the stable. "Don't give him my number."

"Are you crazy?"

"I'm...not a fan of bone-deep, life-long, soul-breaking disappointment."

Nicole stopped mid-step. "What are you talking about?"

"Nic, don't."

"Don't what?" her friend pressed. "Act like you can't have a date? Because I don't buy that, not one bit."

Elise swallowed and let her eyes close. "Who's here to help me off?" she asked, her voice low and stiff.

"My dad's in the stable and Cam, who I pray did not see you on this horse alone." Nicole eyed her and guided Copper toward the open doors. "Don't sell yourself short, E," she whispered. "He obviously liked you."

"He...doesn't know. He couldn't see the harness holding me in place, or the fear in your eyes when you had to step ten feet away. He doesn't know I'm not a... regular girl."

"Well, *I* know you're not a regular girl," Nicole quipped. "I know you're beautiful, hilarious, brilliant, tender-hearted, exuberant, delightful, and—"

"Crippled." Elise blinked hard against the sting in her eyes.

Nicole put her hand on Elise's leg. "Are you going to force me to make your dreams come true again, sister-to-be?"

Elise gave a shaky smile. "You know something?" she asked. "I can't feel your hand on my leg. Not a thing from the top of my thighs to the bottom of my feet. When a man courts a woman, falls in love with a woman, and gets close to a woman, he's going to want her to feel it when he touches her. I can't and never will. So no matter how beautiful or tender or delightful you think I am? I will never be normal or regular or...or..."

Nicole looked up, her eyes swimming in tears. "You feel things in your heart," she said simply. "That's all you need. Let me give him your number."

Elise took a slow, deep breath. What was the worst that could happen? She'd never tried...anything before. She'd never been on a date. She'd never kissed a boy. She'd never been in love.

And this guy was a visitor, so...

"Why the heck not?" she asked on a whisper, as much to herself as Nicole.

Why not? Because she could get her heart shattered as bad as her legs were in an accident fifteen years ago. Well, she'd survived that, so no doubt she could survive a little heartbreak from Alabama.

At least she'd go down smiling.

"'kay," she whispered, closing her eyes so she didn't have to witness Nicole's victory fist pump.

Chapter Four

Red Starling tugged at the fur-trimmed collar of his ill-fitting Santa coat as he trudged up the snowy path from the lodge toward his house. Leftover pasta and a steaming hot cup of coffee waited for him.

A couple of sleigh rides and *everything* hurt.

Well, not his heart. That seemed to be ticking along just fine, but after the nightmare at the ice rink a week ago, he'd been more aware of it than ever before.

His daughters had begged him to give up his Santa gig, which was kind of ironic. A year ago, quitting was all he wanted. But this Christmas? Dressing up as Grumpy—but sometimes nice—Santa when kids were on Jack's sleigh rides kept his mind off that ride in the ambulance.

It also kept him too busy for Drill Sergeant Bertie, his nemesis.

His son-in-law's mother, Roberta Kessler, had shown up the day of Cindy and Jack's wedding and zeroed in on Red like a heat-seeking missile in cross-training shoes. Exercise! Did that woman do anything else?

He'd been warned by Jack that the eighty-six-year-old was the "cardio queen" of her Vermont retirement community, leading chair yoga and calisthenics like she was Jack LaLanne in silver sneakers.

All that woman had heard was "heart scare" and she was off to the races—literally—dragging Red along with her. He'd tried to tell her the docs diagnosed him with heartburn not anything serious. Nope. She was utterly convinced the secret to Red living another twenty years was walking, bending, and, God help him, sit-ups.

So the sleigh rides were sweet relief, but Bertie did seem to have a knack for showing up everywhere.

The last group of riders had been great, though. A bunch of rosy-cheeked tourists from Texas with pockets full of peppermints to feed Copper and some dueling selfie sticks. Still, by the time the final "Merry Christmas, Santa!" echoed through the pines, Red was cooked.

He lumbered past the glittering icicle lights strung over the trees, thinking about that pasta, when Benny buzzed closer on his bright red snow scooter. "Hi, Grandpa!"

"Hey, Benny-bean."

"Look who's still here!"

Olivia, sitting on a disc that looked like a giant Frisbee, whizzed right behind him. "I'm not going to California, Red! My mom's spending Christmas here! She's checking in at the lodge right now! Woohoo!"

She twirled in the snow, making him smile as he resumed his trek. Those kids would be occupied long enough that the pasta could be followed by a few cookies and a nice long nap in his recline—

Oh, no. Oh, *no*! There she was. *The Drill Sergeant.*

Bertie marched in the distance, no doubt about to turn and see Red, which would mean no pasta, no coffee, no cookies, and no nap. Just...movement.

Red froze mid-step, dread washing over him. "Lord above, not now."

Bertie was wearing a puffy vest the color of a pink highlighter and the expression of someone who planned to live to a hundred by sheer force of willpower and walking. Her arms pumped with military precision, her massive fuzzy hat making her look like a bear in fuchsia snow pants.

He knew what was coming. The lecture. The pep talk. The unsolicited advice about heart health and *longevity*. Then...the death march up to Bluebell Crossing and back.

He couldn't do it. Not today.

Moving fast—or as fast as an old man in boots could—he ducked left and hid behind the porch of one of the cabins. He waited, hoping, praying—and heard her marching closer.

Desperate, he climbed onto the porch, grabbed the door handle, and twisted.

Unlocked! Not all of these cabins were rented yet, he knew, since they were rolling out what Cindy called a "soft re-opening"—whatever that was.

Didn't matter. He was safe here.

Warm air greeted him, faintly scented with pine and something lemony from the fresh polish. The place looked brand new. He squinted around approvingly at the recently completed renovations.

Take that, Grand Hyatt. His girls knew what they were doing and his own father, the late, great Owen Starling, would be proud.

The cabin was cozy but modern now—still knotty pine and stone, but with new rugs and soft plaid throws. A sleek gas fireplace flickered in the corner, and the kitchenette gleamed with a white quartz countertop and fresh appliances. The furniture was new but inviting—leather armchairs, wool cushions, and touches of warm wood.

He wandered in a little farther, peeking into the two bedrooms. One was very small, with bunk beds and a hall bath. The other, a little more grand, with an ensuite that had just been added.

Safe for the moment, he stepped into the hall bathroom to see all the changes there. This had been the only bathroom before, with a shower curtain over the tub connected to a water heater that wouldn't moan like ghost and scare guests anymore.

He was about to peek in the mirror to see how ridiculous he looked in the Santa getup when the sound of the front door opening froze him.

"Oh, come on," he whispered. "She *followed* me?"

He closed the bathroom door and listened.

Then he heard women's voices—definitely Gracie, his granddaughter. Was she showing this cabin to Bertie? But when the other woman spoke, it wasn't the voice of his least favorite drill sergeant.

Who was that?

Did it matter? He was Santa, about to be caught breaking and entering.

He stayed quiet, alert, and prayed his stomach didn't growl and give him away, because this was embarrassing.

The voices drifted in from the living room. Gracie's tone was polite but tight, the way she sounded when she was trying very hard to stay civil.

"I think you'll find everything you need. Let me show you the main bedroom and ensuite."

"As long as I can get an Uber to get over to see Marshall, I'm good. Thank you."

"Well, Olivia can stay here with you..."

Oh, it was Olivia's mother, who'd apparently just checked in at the lodge.

"I'm not here just to see Olivia," the woman said, her voice a little sharp as a suitcase rolled by the door, inches from Red.

He winced and waited. Gracie would be furious if she opened the door and found him standing there.

"I'll let you get comfortable, Bianca," Gracie replied, her voice moving toward the front of the cabin. "My mother, MJ, and my Aunt Cindy are available for whatever you need. Goodbye!"

He heard the front door close, the sound of his granddaughter hightailing it away from...Bianca, did she say? He could well imagine Gracie's strawberry-blond hair flying as she made her escape, her whiskey-colored eyes flashing, her freckled cheeks flushed as always. She sure sounded...impatient.

Judging from the way he'd noticed Gracie dancing

with Marshall at the wedding, that impatience was understandable if Bianca was the ex.

But what in tarnation was she doing staying here? Well, Olivia did just tell him she wasn't going to California, so there must have been a change of plans. Not a good one for Gracie, he decided.

He crouched a little, the Santa belt digging into his stomach. How the heck long would he be trapped in here?

He waited, counting silently to ten. Then twenty.

He could still hear movement—soft thuds, the rustle of clothing, a suitcase unzipping again, the flush of the ensuite toilet, then water running.

Red groaned quietly, realizing he'd missed his chance to escape. He couldn't just pop out of the hall bath now— she'd scream bloody murder to find Santa hiding in her cabin.

He eyed the small frosted-glass window behind the toilet. Dang! They'd taken out the old latch he'd installed a hundred years ago and replaced it with permanent glass. Now what?

"Well...I had to call you, Tara," Bianca said, her voice drifting in from outside the door, likely on the phone. "There's been a...tiny hiccup, but it doesn't really change anything. We're still...moving forward."

Just don't move forward into the hall bathroom. Please.

"Well, he wouldn't let me stay at his house," she said to...someone. "I can't imagine why, since there's plenty of room and I could tell by the way he was looking at me that he was so happy I was there. Oh, yes. Over the moon, I'd say."

Really? Very slowly, very quietly, Red lowered himself to sit on top of the toilet seat—glad his daughters had spent the extra money for a substantial potty seat and not one of those flimsy things that buckled like a Tupperware lid.

Stuffing down his qualms about eavesdropping—it wasn't like he had a choice—he sat quietly and listened to the fake-bright voice that some women used when gossiping.

"You are so right, girl, yes!" she cooed, sounding more like Olivia than a grown woman. "Of course, he will spend every chance he can with me. You know he didn't want that divorce." A long pause followed, and for a minute, Red forgot he was hiding out in a bathroom snooping on a guest.

Because this was...interesting.

"I know, I know," she continued, making Red wish she'd put the call on her speaker phone so he could follow the whole thing. "Of course he's still single. He'll never get over me. He looks at me like he's never been around a woman." She gave a high-pitched laugh. "I was always his weakness and I'm gonna be again, Tara. You watch. Once I let him know he can have me again, he won't stand a chance."

Red's blood pressure rose.

"I told you, this is my best shot. My only shot! You're my sister, Tara! Do you want me to go to jail?"

Jail? What would she go to jail for?

"Well, I don't know what they do to people who can't pay their bills. Do you have any earthly idea how high my credit cards are? And rent on that beachfront house? I spent every dime of alimony and it doesn't even begin to touch the debt. That's why I'm here."

Red stood again, cocking his ear to the door, instinctively knowing he had to hear this, but every few words were muffled and impossible for his eighty-three-year-old ears to pick up.

"...No, he wouldn't..." Dang, he didn't get the rest. Then, "Oh, yeah. You never know with Marshall, but..." The rest was unintelligible, so Red leaned closer.

Another bright, girlish laugh followed. "Come on! You remember how it all went. He didn't want a divorce or all that drama. We share a child, Tara. And we will, if things go according to plan, share another."

Wait—what? *Another?* Pretty sure that would be news to Gracie. And Marshall.

"Tara, seriously!" Bianca's voice dropped to a whisper he could barely catch. "No! That's for when this baby's..."

He couldn't decipher the rest. *This* baby? There was a baby? Or she *wanted* a baby?

"No, no. I don't have that much time, hon," she muttered, walking around and doing things that made it impossible for a person to properly eavesdrop.

She gave a vicious laugh. Now *that*, he heard.

"Jonathan was never real, you know that. And he doesn't care if I'm..." A zipper and a thud blocked out the rest of the sentence. "Well, what Marshall doesn't know won't hurt him. And if things line up the way I want, then the whole baby thing won't be so...complicated."

What baby thing? *Line up?* Red felt a buzz of alarm start behind his ears.

"He's generous and he has a soft spot for me," she said, rustling fabric making it hard to hear. "...depends on how he reacts. But I have to move fast." More movement and a suitcase hit the floor. "...like baby needs a daddy, Tara...." She mumbled some more. Then, "It's my best option."

Red's stomach pitched. What baby? Who was "he"? Best option for...*what?*

"It'll be fine," Bianca added. "Olivia will adjust. Kids usually do. And I'm not trying to hurt anybody. I just need things to work out and *fast.*"

His pulse thrummed through his whole body, making him aware of his heart. This kind of stress probably wasn't good for him.

"Oh, my ride's here," she said lightly, passing the bathroom door so close he could hear the clip-clop of heels and the rustle of a jacket. "I'm going into town to see this ridiculous bakery Marshall opened. He'll have to sell it or something, but, trust me, I'm going to pretend it's the most creative, brilliant, and perfect thing I've ever seen." She gave a hoot of a laugh. "Oh, sure, Tara. I'll just put on an apron and sling oatmeal cookies. That'll be the day."

More hyena laughing followed that.

"Of course Olivia will love this. Not that a kid has a say in my life. I'll just remind her that we'll be a family again and everyone will be happy. Especially American Express. Gotta run, babe. Bye!"

Red stayed frozen, waiting for the door to...*there*. Closed.

Finally, he let out his breath.

What in the name of all that was holy did he just hear? A plan or a scheme or the rantings of a madwoman?

Was she pregnant and going to try and pin it on Marshall? It sure sounded that way but...he couldn't be sure. Maybe it was something far more innocent. Maybe he'd misunderstood.

Who could be that calculating?

After a minute, he silently unlatched the bathroom door and looked around the empty cabin, getting a whiff of peppery perfume.

Certain he was alone, he walked to the front window and peeked out, catching sight of a tall woman trudging in the snow toward the lodge. As soon as she rounded the bend of pine trees, he shot out, scrambled off the little porch, and lumbered around the side of the cabin—straight into Bertie Kessler.

"Well, look at you, big guy!" Bertie shouted—she was always so loud. "Sprinting around the place like a man half your age. And dressed as Santa, no less. I'm so impressed."

"Son of a Blitzen," he wheezed, the stress of the last few minutes finally hitting him.

"Did you come out of that cabin?"

"Yes." Red groaned, twisting his aching back.

"What were you doing in there?"

He opened his mouth to tell her he was checking the new electrical but, doggone it—he was disgusted by liars and he refused to be one of them.

"I was avoiding you."

She laughed—a deep, surprised laugh. "Points for honesty, Red. Don't you like me?"

"I don't like speeches about the power of ten thousand steps a day."

Bertie raised an eyebrow. "Oh, we can talk about something else." She slid an arm into his. "While we walk a few thousand of those ten. Come on. Let's go."

He just closed his eyes and said a really, really bad word in his head.

"This way." She tilted her head toward the trail. "You clearly need the exercise—and I could use the company."

He opened his mouth to say no, but the memory of Bianca's smug voice stopped him. He needed time to think, to figure out how to tell Gracie what he'd overheard.

"Fine," he said with a groan. "But if I drop dead halfway, you're explaining it to my granddaughter."

Bertie tugged him onto the trail, eyeing him. "Deal. You look rattled."

"I am." He exhaled a frosty breath. "Sometimes people surprise you in the worst ways."

Bertie nodded slowly. "And sometimes they surprise you in the best ways, too."

"Maybe," he said quietly. "But not that often."

They walked on in companionable silence, which Red appreciated because he knew he couldn't tell anyone what he'd heard. It would implode in the worst imaginable way.

Just as they turned the bend near the frozen creek, he heard Benny's giggle, and saw Olivia dive out from behind a massive tree.

"How did you find me?" Olivia squealed.

It was the beautiful sound of two little kids innocently playing Hide 'n' Seek with no idea their world was about to be ruined.

He couldn't let it happen. He couldn't.

"Hi, Grandpa!" Benny waved. "Hi, Miss Bertie!"

He saw Benny and Olivia exchange a high-five, laughter floating on the air as they jumped on their snow toys and took off, leaving joy in their wake.

If what he'd heard was right and that woman was planning on dragging Marshall and Olivia away from here...well, that couldn't happen. Benny had a lot to lose if his best friend left. And Gracie would be heartbroken.

No one—*no one*—was going to hurt Red Starling's family.

He just had no idea how to stop her.

Chapter Five

Gracie

G racie eased a golden and delicious tray of cream puffs from the oven, then checked the day's receipts so far. All good...and about to get better.

Slipping into her office, she closed the door to change for her late afternoon date.

She'd grabbed an ice-blue sweater with a pearl-trimmed collar and her favorite black jeans, which felt perfect for walking around town, grabbing dinner, and spending time deepening their budding romance.

Barely able to wipe the smile from her face, she freshened up, re-applied her makeup, and brushed out her strawberry blond hair. Adding some jewelry she never wore at work and slipping into low-heeled boots, she glance at the full-length mirror in the powder room, happy with the final result.

Taking a deep breath, she shut down her computer, grabbed a small bag, and stepped out into the kitchen.

"You sure you don't mind covering for me until close, Amanda?" Gracie asked her manager as she passed.

"Not a bit, Gracie." A talented baker and a good friend, Amanda was by far her most reliable employee. "I've got the pies handled, too."

"You're the best. And if it stays this slow, feel free to close up early." Gracie leaned her palms on the counter, looking around at the tables, for once not doing a head count on the customers.

Not today. She didn't want to think about work today, just the date that would start in ten minutes.

A couple rose from a table near the window and Gracie automatically pushed off the counter to clear the cups and plates they'd left behind.

"I got it," Amanda said, putting her hand on Gracie's arm. "You'll get chocolate on that beautiful top."

The door dinged, opening to new customers, so Gracie smiled at Amanda. "I'll fill this order, then. Thanks."

She turned to greet the customer, blinking in shock at the sight of Bianca Hampton, who was intently perusing the glass display, eyes on Amanda's last batch of buttercream cupcakes.

"Oh. Hello."

"Hi." Bianca didn't look up, shifting a few shopping bags—all from high-end boutiques on Main Street—from one hand to the other. "I'll take a red velvet cupcake. And a cream puff. Oh, throw in that chocolaty ganache tart thing, too."

"That's Olivia's favorite," Gracie told her.

The other woman finally looked up, sucking in a breath. For a heartbeat or two, she stared over the glass display case, her expression blank enough that Gracie thought she didn't remember meeting this morning or riding to Snowberry Lodge together.

"Oh, it's you," Bianca said. "Uh...Gloria?" she guessed, making a face. "Sorry, I'm terrible with names."

"Gracie," she supplied. "It's nice to see you here. Is Olivia out there, or..." She looked around. "With you?"

"She stayed at the lodge to play with her little friend."

"Benny. My son." Gracie tried to smile politely, but struggled. Had Bianca already ditched Olivia? Hours after arriving?

"Right, Benny. I just..." She threw a look over her shoulder in the general direction of Craving Clean. "Marshall insisted I come see his cute little...endeavor. After that, I had to do a little shopping but now I'm starving. And I can't go to Marshall's because..." She made an embarrassed wince. "There's not a decent thing to eat at that place and I have a sweet tooth for some reason. I thought Sugarfall meant this might be a candy store. It's like his, though. A bakery?"

"Only with sugar," Gracie deadpanned, ignoring "he insisted I come" and "cute little endeavor."

"Exactly what I need." Bianca gave a self-conscious laugh. "I know I shouldn't, but"— she lifted the bags— "retail therapy is best ended on a sugar high, I like to say."

So she'd visited his store, shopped for clothes, and now was hitting up Sugarfall—all *without* the daughter she'd flown here to see?

"Well, choose whatever you like," Gracie said, trying to keep her jumbled thoughts straight. "You can always keep it in the fridge in your cabin and have a midnight snack." She couldn't resist adding, "With Olivia, who really does love the ganache. Be sure to ask her where it gets its shine."

Bianca gave a flat smile that didn't reach her eyes. "Where what gets...what?"

"The ganache," Gracie said, hating that she felt a blush bloom under the surface of her cheeks. Why? Bianca was the one who knew nothing about her own daughter's love of science. *She* should be blushing. "She'll explain how the sugar crystals melt at a certain temperature to make it..." Her voice faded out in the face of the clueless expression Bianca wore.

Gracie swallowed. "In a box to go, then, Bianca?"

Bianca glanced at the freshly bused table by the window...the window that looked right at Craving Clean. "Give me a decaf with that, so I can stay here."

Really? She was going to stay? Which meant she'd see Marshall in less than ten—

"How long have you worked here?" Bianca asked, eyeing her phone as if the answer didn't really matter but she had to make small talk.

Gracie carefully placed the red velvet cupcake on a plate, leaving room for the other desserts. "I opened Sugarfall when Benny was five, so six years now."

"You...own it?" Bianca's brows shot up.

"I do," Gracie said. "I'm a pastry chef and this is my shop."

"Huh." Bianca looked hard at Gracie, clearly considering her in a new light. Not the dog walker, not the friend's mom, but a business owner. The slightest grudging look of interest flickered in the woman's topaz eyes. "Lucky you—working right across the street from my...from Marshall."

How should Gracie answer that? How would she respond to that if she *didn't* have a date with the man in less than five minutes? Diplomatically, that's how.

"Well, I've certainly lost a few calorie-conscious customers, but that's fine."

"Is it?" the other woman challenged. "I mean, I can't believe people would eat his raw honey oatmeal horrors when there's...*this*."

"Don't knock the honey and oatmeal," she said, forcing a smile. "Marshall's incredibly talented in the kitchen."

Bianca widened her eyes, looking down. "And elsewhere," she murmured.

Gracie's cheeks were pretty much a five-alarm fire with that comment, but Bianca didn't see as she whipped out a credit card, looked at it and stuck it back in her wallet. With a huffed sigh, she grabbed a twenty-dollar bill.

"Keep the change, Grace."

Gracie just kept on smiling and thanked her, resisting the urge to mention that tipping wasn't necessary. "I'll bring you coffee. Sugar and cream?"

"Yes, please. Lots of both."

She whisked away to the table with a tray of treats, that white coat fluttering in her wake. Gracie turned to get the coffee, but Amanda was back.

"I got it, boss." She jabbed a light elbow into Gracie's side. "You go...wherever you're going looking so pretty."

Glancing at the front window, she spotted Marshall crossing the street, wearing a leather bomber jacket over dark trousers. He'd changed, too, which really made her feel good.

But...what about Bianca? The woman was halfway through the cupcake, eyes on her phone. Maybe they could get out unseen?

Marshall pulled open the door and strolled in, dark eyes leveled on Gracie as she slipped out from behind the counter. She'd barely come around when he lifted both hands to give her a hug.

"Hey, gorgeous," he said in a low voice. "You ready?"

She took a hesitant step closer, inhaling sharply, entirely unsure how to handle the situation. He didn't give her a choice, closing the space with a hug that could have been between friends or colleagues...or a couple.

As she lightly hugged him back, Gracie glanced to her right to find Bianca staring right at them.

She stiffened and inched back. "You'll never guess who's—"

"Marshall?" Bianca rose and came toward them, her long legs eating up the black-and-white checkered floor in less than four strides.

He whipped around, his whole relaxed posture instantly on alert.

"Oh...Bianca. I thought you were..." He looked beyond her, then around. "Do you have Olivia?"

"No, no. She's still at that...that Snowbird place." She glanced at Gracie, her gaze lingering with a whole different level of interest. "Your mother's little lodge."

Was everything *little* to this woman? Certainly not her ego.

"And you're just..." Marshall looked confused. "Here?"

"Well, I hit up a few cute stores and then I saw this precious bakery. You didn't mention that Olivia's friend's mom owns this place."

"We didn't talk about it."

"I'm surprised you didn't say something while I was taking a tour of your bakery," Bianca said, pressing her hands together. "Gracie, have you seen it? The way he makes healthy food look so good and all the busy things in the kitchen. He's come so far from the football field and I'm so proud of him."

Gracie managed not to roll her eyes, but it wasn't easy. Every word that came out of her mouth sounded disingenuous.

Marshall replied with a quick, tight smile. "We should go," he said to Gracie, reaching out his hand for hers and making zero effort to hide...well, anything.

Bianca's gaze dropped to their joined hands, then rose back to Gracie's face.

"How cute. You blush." She trilled a laugh. "And here I thought you were the dog walker."

Gracie didn't have any idea what to say, but Marshall put his arm around her and guided her to the door.

"Don't leave Olivia alone for too long, Bianca," he said as they passed by.

Gracie snagged her jacket from a hook near the door, but he slipped it out of her hands and held it up for her to slide into. As she did, he leaned close to her ear and whispered, "Not that it could be any chillier outside than it is in here."

She threw a smile over her shoulder and let him lead her out to the sidewalk. They stood there for a moment while she zipped her coat and they both slipped on gloves.

"I certainly wasn't expecting her," Gracie said.

He exhaled. "Neither was I. She showed up at Craving Clean a few hours ago, poking around, talking to me...being weird."

"Weird?"

He closed his eyes as if he didn't like what he had to say. "She's up to something," he told her. "I don't know what her angle is, but she always has one and she is definitely up to something."

"Maybe she's considering asking for more time with Olivia," Gracie suggested. "You know, a change in custody? More time in L.A.?"

He shook his head. "Just the opposite." Taking her hand and tucking it protectively into the crook of his arm, he walked to the crosswalk, paused to check for traffic, and then walked them across. "She wants time with me, not Olivia."

"Maybe she...wants you back."

He snorted. "That's not happening." He slowed his

step once they'd crossed, looking down at Gracie. "First things first, Gracie McBride. You look spectacular."

She felt a huge smile pull. "Thank you."

"And this date—a little time in town, and a nice dinner at The Lakehouse Grill—is not going to be spoiled by my ex and her secret agenda."

A secret agenda? How intriguing. But before she could ask, he took her hands in his and drew her closer.

"Let's forget she's here and concentrate on what matters—our time together." He punctuated that with the lightest kiss on her forehead. "I've literally been counting the minutes until I could see you."

She resisted the urge to giggle, but did *not* resist the need to stand on the toes of her boots and respond with a lightning-fast kiss on his lips. "For a guy who doesn't do sugar, that was just about the sweetest thing I ever heard."

He laughed and hugged her, keeping his arm tightly around her as they strode down the sidewalk...in full view of that window table.

She didn't know what Bianca's secret agenda was, but right then, she didn't care.

THE NEXT MORNING, Gracie woke up smiling.

Not the dainty, demure smile of a shy pastry chef who'd written off the possibility of falling in love again as the stuff of romance novels. No, this was the wide and wonderful Cheshire cat grin of a woman who suddenly believed that love wasn't just possible…it was right around the corner.

With a shiver, she climbed out of bed and pulled on her fluffiest slippers and coziest robe, inhaling the scents of bacon and coffee that floated up from the kitchen.

"God bless you, Red," she whispered, eternally grateful her grandfather was an early riser.

She lingered momentarily, gazing out at a snowy world, the rooflines of Snowberry Lodge visible as nothing but a white-on-white blur from this second floor bedroom.

As alluring as the siren call of coffee and bacon might be, she wasn't quite ready to shake the haze of happiness that had clung to her since last night. She could still taste a long and lovely goodnight kiss, the memory spreading warmth all the way to her toes.

Was that her favorite moment of the night? When Marshall wrapped her in his arms outside of her car, with snowflakes melting on the collar of his coat while she melted in his embrace?

Or was it when he reached across the linen-covered table at The Lakehouse Grill and thumbed her knuckles tenderly, looking at her like she was something rare and wonderful.

Maybe it was when they slipped into a Christmas store and picked a few new ornaments for his tree, the two of them planning a decorating date in a few days.

There'd been so many perfect moments, she felt like

she'd been in her own blurred movie montage of laughter, kisses, and deep conversation.

She didn't care that Bianca had seen them leave together. Nor did she care that half the town probably knew by now. Right now, Gracie didn't care what anyone thought.

She floated downstairs, her fingers dancing along the banister that had supported three generations—four, if she counted Benny—of Starlings who'd lived in this fine old farmhouse on the edge of the Snowberry property.

Would she leave this house if she fell in love and married Marshall? She froze mid-step as the shocking thought hit her hard.

Not that it was *that* shocking—although Marshall hadn't used the M word or the L word or any forever term, he had made it abundantly clear he wasn't...what was the expression? Window-shopping.

So, if they got serious and did get married, would she and Benny move in with—

"I thought I heard a customer." Red poked his head out of the kitchen door. "G'morning, sunshine. How are you?" The question came out equal parts teasing and curious.

Of course, he knew she'd had a date last night, but this was all new territory for Gracie and Red. The last man she'd "dated" was Sam, a loser who got her pregnant and then hauled out of town.

Since then, there'd been no man in her life but the one she was raising. How would her opinionated grandfather feel about that change?

Guess she was about to find out.

"Morning," she said dreamily, snagging a piece of bacon as she passed. "You're up early."

"Old men don't sleep much," he said, flipping another strip. "Especially when some lunatic named Bertie texted me at five a.m. to—get this—do a sunrise power-walk."

Gracie choked. "She...texted you? How did she get your number?"

"Probably from Cindy, who I'm officially disowning today." He stirred the batter and eyed her over his rimless specs that, along with the beard, made it look like Santa himself was at work in the kitchen. "You look... happy."

Gracie leaned against the counter, trying not to grin too big. "I *am* happy."

He poured a cup of coffee, sliding it toward her like a bartender. "That's good. That's real good."

There was something about the way he said it—like the words had splinters—that made her tilt her head. Maybe he'd already thought of the logistics if this brand-new relationship went anywhere. Red couldn't live here alone, could he?

Nope, not an option.

She went to the fridge for cream, considering just how much to tell him. Better he know now that this was happening. Plus, she could never hide anything from her grandfather.

"We had the best night, Red. I mean, really wonderful. We walked around town, looked at the snow globes, listened to that street violinist near the square. And then dinner at The Lakehouse."

"Fancy," Red murmured.

"Not too fancy," she said, taking a sip of coffee and sliding into her seat at the kitchen table. "Perfect, actually. We talked about everything—family, work, faith, life. He told me he doesn't really date just to date. He's looking for something real. And he thinks...maybe that's me."

Red slid her a look that was just dubious enough to make her heart fall.

"No? You don't think so?"

"Me?" he scoffed. "Gracie girl, I don't get a say in your personal life."

"You have a say in my everything life," she quipped. "Please, feel free to opine. Or do you think someone like Marshall would never love someone like me?"

Her grandfather wiped his hands on a dish towel, his eyes narrowing slightly. "What's that supposed to mean, someone like you?"

"You know," she said softly. "I'm not...outgoing. I like to bake and read and am not really..." She wanted to say "beautiful" but Marshall had made her feel utterly gorgeous last night, and he'd meant it. "I'm not like, say, his ex."

He snorted. "Thank the good Lord for that."

"Have you met her?"

"Yeah, I, uh, bumped into her on the property."

"She's beautiful, right?"

He turned away, concentrating on the bacon sizzling

in the pan. "Well, see, now, everyone defines that differ-ently. Cora was beautiful."

Gracie smiled, thinking of her dear grandmother. "Completely," she agreed.

"But some people are just diamonds on the outside, and nothing but...coal dust on the inside." He turned, his eyes looking...pained. "Gracie girl, any man who doesn't see you as a catch needs his head examined."

She smiled, touched by the comment but frowning as she searched his face.

"You okay?" she asked. "You look...worried."

"Nah," he said quickly, waving it off. "Just listening and thinking about...it all."

What all? "Do you not like Marshall, Red?"

He hesitated just a second too long. Then he shook his head. "I like him fine. Good man. Seems steady."

"But?" she pressed gently.

He started to say something—she saw it, the flicker of words right behind his lips—then footsteps padded down the hall.

Benny appeared in his pajamas, hair sticking up, glasses askew, phone in hand. "Mom? Guess what?"

"What, sweetheart?"

He plopped onto a stool. "Olivia texted me. They're going skiing today. Her mom, her dad, and her. The three of them."

"Bianca is skiing?" Red asked, sounding oddly surprised by that.

"Well, she doesn't want to ski but she wants 'the

family experience'"—Benny used air quotes—"'and a picture for Instagram."

Gracie froze for half a breath. "Oh," she said lightly. "How fun. I...I..." Never heard a word about skiing today, she thought.

Why wouldn't Marshall mention that? Or maybe he didn't know. Or it had to do with...what had Marshall called it? Bianca's secret agenda? What could that possibly be, other than the obvious ploy to win him back.

She forced a smile. "That's...nice. Family time."

Benny nodded, abandoning the phone to attack the bacon. She waited for Red to tell him to hold off until the eggs were ready, but when she looked across the kitchen, her grandfather was staring out the window.

His gaze was steady, his bearded jaw set the way it was when he was digging deep for the answer to a particularly hard crossword clue.

"What is it, Red?" she asked softly.

He shook his head and held up a hand as if to stave off any more questions. "Nothing. Just—be careful, Gracie girl. People are full of surprises. Sometimes good ones, sometimes the other kind."

Her throat tightened, but she managed another smile. "You don't have to worry about me, Red. I'm not sixteen."

He smiled faintly, the corners of his mouth tugging down as he laid bacon on a paper towel. "You're my granddaughter. That's my job."

"Your job is to be Grumpy Santa on the sleigh," Benny said. "Any chance I could suit up in my elf costume and go with, Grandpa? With Olivia gone and school on break, I don't have anything to do."

"You can be my bodyguard all day."

"Cool!" He stood up and squared his little pajama-clad shoulders. "Just call me McBride. Benedict McBride."

"You need a bodyguard?" Gracie asked, laughing at Benny's bad James Bond imitation.

"Yes, because I have a stalker. That Sergeant Bertie won't let me have five minutes of peace without slapping something on my wrist to measure things that have no right being measured. I don't know what my...my *vox* is and I don't care!"

Gracie laughed. "I think Uncle Jack's mom has a crush on you, Red."

"What?" Benny almost spit out his OJ. "That's so gross, Mom. Eww. They're, like, a thousand years old."

Red turned from the stove and fried him with a look. "Not a day over nine hundred, Benny-bean. Now, Gracie...don't you let anything steal that happiness you came downstairs with. Just...be careful."

The warning—repeated for a second time—gave her pause. She wrapped her hands around her mug, trying to hold onto the warmth. What could he mean? What had put that worried look in Red Starling's eyes?

And then it became crystal clear, just as her grandfather looked around the old house with a slightly...lost expression. Of *course*. He knew if she got serious with Marshall, it could mean she and Benny would move out and leave him in this big house all alone.

That's why he looked a little worried and doubtful, and understandably so.

She stood to refill her coffee and, as she passed, put a reassuring hand on his back. "Great breakfast, Red." She patted him with love. "Don't know where we'd be without you."

He just gave her a sad smile and she made a mental note that whatever happened to her, she'd never abandon her dear, sweet grandfather.

Chapter Six

Elise

The best thing about living alone, Elise had decided, was the freedom to talk to herself without anyone thinking she was crazy.

She leaned close to her bathroom mirror, applying the faintest shimmer of rose-gold eyeshadow and saying to her reflection, "You are calm, confident, and absolutely *fine.*"

The mirror, of course, didn't argue.

Her one-bedroom apartment—the ground-floor, wheelchair-accessible unit in the student housing building of Great Basin Veterinary Institute—was flooded with late-morning light.

She'd lived here nearly a year, long enough to create a space that reflected the joy of finally being an independent adult woman spreading her wings—or wheels—and experiencing life.

Family photos filled one wall. A shelf near her desk overflowed with succulents and orchids. The window ledge held a vase of bright fake daisies because daisies made her happy.

A fuzzy pink blanket was tossed over the bottom of

the bed, and the faint scent of coffee and lavender floated through the air.

It wasn't much, but it was hers. Her home, her world, her freedom. Yes, there were some grab bars, wide doorways, and low kitchen counters, but to the untrained eye, this was a girlie-girl's beautiful living space.

And she was the girlie-girl living in it.

With a smile, she added another coat of mascara, tilted her head, and gazed at the reflection. Her blond hair tumbled in waves around her face, her makeup on point from shadow to lips, and the creamy soft sweater she'd chosen to wear with jeans flattered her coloring. Jewelry jingled as she adjusted her earrings—colorful hoops shaped like tiny horseshoes.

She was ready.

And she was absolutely, one hundred percent certain that Wade Reynolds would see her and think...*Yikes. She's in a wheelchair.*

Then that brief flicker of interest he'd shown when she was on horseback a few days ago—when he'd laughed at her jokes and looked her right in the eyes with an easy, confident grin—would vanish.

Elise Hale had conquered a lot of difficult challenges in her life and she'd faced her share of adversity. But she'd never—not once, not ever—attracted a man. At least not one who would be up to her excruciating standards, set by her one-in-a-million brother, Cam.

A man, Elise knew, would have no interest in a paraplegic, no matter how pretty she was, how effervescent and funny, or how great a vet she would be. Once Wade

Reynolds, handsome Southern oncology vet with eyes so green they looked bedazzled, realized she was crippled, it would be all over.

He'd politely tour the campus, make friendly convo, and zip back to Park City with a "see ya around, Elise" on the way out.

She knew that, but did it stop her from letting fantasy-level hopes build with each minute that the clock ticked closer to his arrival? No, it did not. Because Elise was normal in every way except for the severed nerve that said her legs would never move or feel anything.

And that just *wasn't* normal.

She capped her lip gloss, straightened, and rolled into the living room, reminding herself how far she'd come.

A year ago, she'd applied to GBVI on a lark, certain she wouldn't get in.

She'd nearly had to bail on the final interview with the dean, but darling Nicole had brought her here and that sealed the deal.

Now, a year later, Elise was a thriving, happy, popular twenty-five-year-old. She took classes, had "patients" in the animal hospital, and had been given the opportunity to manage the Live Nativity project.

She could get around almost as well as any other student—able to use her strong and steady arms to lift herself from bed to chair to toilet to bath. She could dress and dress well. She favored long flowy skirts that were easy to get on and off, excruciatingly cute tops with no shortage of bling and a little cleavage, and UGG boots. She could also shop, cook, study, work on animals, hang with friends, and be an excellent graduate student obtaining a DVM.

So, basically, she was living her best life. Which, on dark nights alone in her bed, really meant the "best life for a girl who'd never walk, dance, ski, or run into the arms of a loving husband."

On her lap, her phone buzzed and lit with a text.

Wade Reynolds: *I'm outside :)*

"Here we go," she muttered. "Pop goes the truth bubble the minute I roll out there."

Would she see the surprise and disappointment in his eyes, or would he hide it? Would he joke about it or suddenly go sympathetic and serious, asking how it had happened? Or would he do what so many people tried—and usually failed—to do? To pretend that a wheelchair made no difference.

Time to find out what the Alabama hottie was made of.

Pulling on her poncho, she took a steadying breath, rolled toward the door and left the apartment, her wheels whispering softly against the polished hallway floor. The residence hall of the vet institute smelled like cinnamon rolls from someone's toaster oven and the faint disinfectant of freshly cleaned tile.

When she reached the glass double doors at the front, she spotted him right away.

Wade Reynolds stood in the crisp winter sunlight, hands in his pockets, looking around the campus like he belonged there. Under a puffer vest, his flannel shirt was rolled to the elbows, faded jeans over scuffed boots.

He had a square jaw, dark hair just long enough to curl above his collar, and that same easy smile she'd tried not to replay in her mind since meeting him. No cowboy hat this time, but somehow that made him even more attractive.

In fact, he was so good-looking it almost hurt. Well, it would hurt when those pretty green eyes slid over the chair that confined her and clouded in disappointment.

She waved her hand over the auto open button and rolled out into the sunshine to the pavilion where he stood. He turned, angled his head, and held out his arms like...well, like she could run into them.

"There's the cowgirl."

His eyes flicked down, just for a heartbeat, taking in the chair. But there was no disappointment, surprise, or curiosity. Just a smile.

Not a pity smile. Not a startled, *oh-gosh-I-don't-know-what-to-say* smile. Just a warm and genuine smile that took him from a solid nine to an eleven. And a half.

"Hey, there, Elise," he said, walking toward her. "Nice to see you again."

She blinked, thrown.

"Hi," she managed, laughing more out of relief than any bubble of joy. Okay. Maybe a little bubble of joy. "Welcome to Great Basin Veterinary Institute."

He crouched so they were eye level—unconsciously respectful and close enough that she could see his crystalline green eyes were fringed with dark lashes that came together as he squinted at her. "I can't believe this is real."

Her heart dropped. Of course it was real. Did he

think she used a wheelchair as a fashion accessory, like lashes or nails or a high-end purse?

"It's...real," she said, not surprised that her throat was tight.

"It's nuts!" He made a sweeping gesture. "The mountains, the view, this incredible campus. Please don't tell me you get so used to the beauty of this place that you don't notice it anymore."

She took in a slow breath and recalibrated her initial reaction. Then she looked around at the quaint brick and stone buildings, the open, snow-dusted quad with a few students meandering with backpacks and serious "finals week" expressions. Rugged mountains on either side tucked the campus into a thriving community that included homes, businesses, and plenty of ranches and farmland.

"Sometimes you just need to see something through someone else's eyes," she said, her gaze landing on him—a sight as attractive as the setting. "So, thanks for that perspective."

"Hey, I live in Alabama, where it's flat and hot and... nice." He shrugged. "But it's not this. I think I've spent every minute since my plane landed just staring at those mountains and that sky. I love Utah!"

She giggled at his enthusiasm, agreeing with him.

When were they going to talk about it? Maybe she had to break the ice.

"I count my blessings every day," she added, squeezing the armrests secretly as she chose humor to do the job. "I pinch myself to make sure I'm not dreaming. Although, south of my hips, I don't feel it."

His brows lifted, maybe a little amused, maybe surprised. But still no comment, no pity, no sigh, or the inevitable questions that usually started with, "Were you born this way?"

Nothing. He just grinned and stuffed his hands in the pockets of his Levi's. "And it's so sunny, you don't even notice the cold," he continued, like he worked for the Eagle Mountain tourist commission. "Although I like that cape thing you're wearing."

Finally, she let out a soft laugh. "Are we going to address the elephant in the room?" She gave a quick gesture toward the chair. "The rolling elephant."

"You treat elephants at this school? Because I have to admit that in my years of training, I've yet to work on an elephant."

She angled her head, not sure where to go with this. "Wade."

He eyed her for a moment. "Did you think I didn't know?"

"I...well, yeah. I was on a horse when we met."

"I'm Southern, not dumb," he joked. When she didn't laugh, he tipped his head. "I saw the harness and sensed Nicole was as much an escort as a friend. After you left, I noticed a ramp in the stables. Bein' the math genius I am, I put two and two together and came up with..."

"Girl in a wheelchair," she finished when he didn't.

"I was thinking more along the lines of smokeshow who obviously doesn't let life beat her down, is probably stronger than I ever will be, and has the same heart for animals that I do."

She felt her jaw loosen at the litany of compliments. Did he say...*smokeshow?*

"Wow. No one ever..." She couldn't even finish, so she just closed her eyes. "Sometimes I hate that harness, but not today."

"Why would you hate it?" he asked.

"Hate is the wrong word. I love that it allows me to ride, I just wish I could get on the horse without two men and a prayer helping me, and that I could actually feel secure enough to ride alone. But thank you, Wade, for all your compliments."

He smiled. "I mean it." Then he looked past her toward the buildings. "Now, I can't wait to see this bee-*yoo*-tiful school and the tour better include animals. Also, coffee. I drove from Park City in my uncle's rented SUV and was so distracted by nature's handiwork that I never stopped. Is there caffeine around?"

"In a painfully cute coffee shop called the Canine Café," she told him, her heart lifting at his utterly wonderful attitude. Classy, positive, easy.

Where did this guy come from?

"Canine Café?" He snorted. "Yes, please."

"Right on the other side of the quad," she said, giving her wheels a push.

He kept up with her, giving her no chance to ponder this unexpected turn of events as he peppered her with questions. And he didn't offer to push, which she *loved*.

There was nothing worse than being wheeled when she could do it herself.

They moved along the main sidewalk that connected the teaching barn to the classroom wing, their breath visible in the frosty air. She pointed out the rehab building—a low, modern structure with glass walls and a pool used for equine hydrotherapy.

"That's where we do physical therapy and conditioning," she said. "The horses love it. The goats...not so much."

"Goats never cooperate," Wade said with mock solemnity. "I did a rotation once where a goat bit my shoelace and removed my shoe smack in the middle of surgery prep."

She laughed. "That's a goat for you."

"I was washed and ready, so I had to finish the procedure wearing one shoe like a sad pirate."

She giggled, wheeling alongside him as they reached the Canine Café.

"I highly recommend the caramel latte," she said.

"Two of those coming right up."

While he jogged ahead to the window and ordered drinks, she waited, soaking in the quiet of the coffee shop on winter break. A moment later, he returned, holding one cup out to her. "Caramel latte for the future Dr. Hale."

"Three more years until I get the title," she said, adding her thanks for the coffee. "But you're way ahead of me."

"I feel like I've been in school forever," he said,

blowing into the hole in the plastic lid. "I really considered just getting the DVM and starting to work, but the oncology department lured me in."

"What did they put on that bait? Gold? Oncology is three more years and a residency, right?"

"I lost count," he joked, holding the door to go back outside. "I've now done four years undergrad, four years DVM, the rotating internship, then three years in oncology. I'll be thirty next year and I haven't actually held a real job."

"I haven't either, and I'm twenty-five. Like I said, way ahead of me."

"What did you do after you finished school?" he asked. "You must have waited before going to grad school."

"I got my undergrad degree online," she explained. "And I lived with my parents out in Heber City, which is not too far from Park City. I didn't work, because..." She gave her armrests a tap. "Mom and Dad didn't think that was a good idea. Then I found out about this program and..."

"Bucked the odds," he said, that Alabama accent even sweeter with his smile. "See? I was right about you. Li'l blond Superwoman."

"Hardly." But the compliment tickled her right down to the toes she couldn't feel.

As they sipped their coffee and continued the tour, he asked about her coursework, the student clinics, the kinds of cases they saw. He told her about his oncology residency—how he'd stayed up for forty hours once to help a golden retriever through chemo complications, sure they'd lose him in the middle of the night.

"He made it," Wade said, eyes soft. "His family sent me a Christmas card with his pawprint."

"That's so sweet," she said, genuinely moved.

"I still have it," he added. "That's what makes it all worthwhile, right? The dog that lives, the cat that pulls through. I even treated a ferret with bone cancer. I love it, actually."

The way he said it—matter-of-fact but full of heart—made her pulse skip.

"I do, too," she admitted. "I haven't saved any lives yet, but just the fundamentals are satisfying in this business. And there's so much to learn!"

"That never stops," he said as they passed a fenced field where about six dogs were running around like controlled chaos in the cold.

"That's the therapy pack," Elise explained. "We take them to children's hospitals and nursing homes. They're like four-legged antidepressants."

"I love that," he said. "What about the Live Nativity? Where will that be?"

"Right here on the quad on Christmas Eve," she said. "They're going to start building the stable next week and I have to make sure all the actors—animals and people— are ready."

"My guess is the animals will be easier than the people," he said with a laugh.

"No doubt about it, except for maybe the goats. Oh,

and the donkey is a little bit arrogant. I mean, for a donkey."

"Right? Someone tell him he's not a horse," Wade joked.

"We also have a new sheep who might steal the show."

"What an awesome thing to get to do for Christmas," he said. "Can I help? Or at least meet the four-legged stars?"

Was he always so infectiously enthusiastic? She adored that about him. With each happy observation or upbeat tone, she felt more at ease. How could she not? He made everything seem like an adventure.

"Of course. They're in the barn. Come on." She pivoted in a 180-degree turn that she'd executed a million times. But the move had him slowing his step and looking down at her with an unreadable expression. "What is it?" she asked.

"Nothing. You're just...agile and fearless."

"Few would call me agile," she said with a dry laugh. "And fearless? I don't know about that. I'm afraid of a lot of things."

"Like what?" he asked.

She looked up at him, catching the sun glinting on his dark hair and the gleam in his green eyes.

"Just the usual things..." But right then, she couldn't imagine a single thing she was afraid of...except falling so hard for this man she might as well wheel herself off a cliff right now.

He leaned a little closer. "I knew it."

What did he know? That right then and right there, she was developing a crush the size of the mountains in the distance? That her usual wit and charm just dried up in the face of this handsome creature? That she couldn't see, think, or roll straight in front of him?

"Knew what?" she asked, her voice tentative as she braced for the response.

"You're fearless, cowgirl. I love that."

He loved that? And had a nickname for her?

For once, she was happy to be in this chair, so she didn't wobble on her weak knees.

"Let's go to the barn," she managed to say, thumbing in that general direction. "You can meet my crew."

As they made their way toward the barn that housed the Nativity animals, Elise realized she'd stopped thinking about her chair entirely. He didn't slow down for her or speed up. He didn't hover or overcompensate.

He just...matched her.

And for someone who'd spent half her life feeling like everyone either pitied her or wanted to fix her, that felt like a miracle.

INSIDE THE SECONDARY barn tucked to the side of the campus, Elise and Wade were greeted by a soft chorus of snorts and bleats beneath the hum of heat lamps. Light fell through the high windows in narrow, golden shafts, catching bits of dust and straw that floated like snow.

"These are our Nativity volunteers," Elise said, rolling down the center aisle.

A donkey lifted his head from a feed bucket and brayed, then meandered out the other door to an outdoor pan. Two goats butted playfully behind a swinging door. In the last stall, a new arrival stood apart from the rest—a white-faced ewe with coarse wool and a tentative, searching look.

"This lovely lady came in yesterday," Elise said. "A farmer over in Cedar Valley offered to lend some of his flock for the pageant, but he wasn't sure about this one. Said she seemed... off. Not sick, exactly—just not herself."

Wade stopped beside the rail, studying the animal. "Mind if I step in?"

"Go ahead. She's gentle."

He unlatched the stall door and crouched low, letting the ewe sniff his sleeve. The animal hesitated, then inched forward, trusting.

After a minute, he glanced back at Elise. "You notice her eye?"

"The right one is a little swollen," she said, wheeling in. She'd noticed the skin around the eye was slightly raised and roughened, like pale coral under the lashes. "I thought it was a scratch. Maybe she bumped something in transport. There's no discharge, no fever."

"It's not an infection," he murmured. He touched lightly at the wool near her temple, careful not to startle her. "See this plaque here? Almost chalky?"

Elise leaned forward, studying the spot. It wasn't

large, but there was something unsettling about it—the way the light caught the uneven texture, the way the ewe blinked more slowly with that eye.

"I've seen something like this before," Wade said. "But never in a sheep. Cattle, yes, but sheep aren't common cases."

"What is it?" she asked.

"Could be nothing, like you said, but it could be ocular squamous cell carcinoma."

She drew back sharply. "Cancer?"

"Hard to say without a biopsy. But it's the right shape, the right color." He ran a hand along the ewe's neck, his voice gentling. "Poor girl. Maybe that's why the farmer sent her along—hoping someone here might take a look."

Elise's throat tightened. "It would make sense if he can't afford treatment, but we don't even have an oncology department."

"Well, I'm here and happy to give my advice, for what it's worth."

Something in the way he said it—steady and sure—made her think it might be worth a lot.

"What's the treatment if it is carcinoma?" she asked.

"First, it needs to be confirmed with a biopsy, since the best option is to put your mind at ease. If it's positive, I can help you put together a treatment plan."

"What might that be?"

"It's early, but my guess would be minor excision and, if it hasn't spread, cryotherapy. I've handled worse." His smile softened. "If it's caught early, it's treatable. Especially if it hasn't spread into the orbit. Not a complicated treatment, but the sooner the better."

Elise let out a breath. "Then she came to the right place."

The ewe gave a low, wavering bleat, as if agreeing. Wade chuckled, resting a palm against her shoulder. "What's her name?"

Elise shook her head. "The farmer didn't say, but he did comment that she'd been in shambles for a while, whatever that means."

Wade's eyes warmed as he looked at the animal. "All right then, Shambles." He patted her again. "Let's see if we can put your life, and eye, back together again."

"Shambles?" She laughed. "I love it."

He turned to smile at Elise. Crouched down as he was, he had to look up at her. Their gazes met, the air thick with straw dust and the faint rhythm of the ewe's breathing. For a heartbeat or two, neither of them moved.

Finally, Wade straightened. "Let me know what I can do to help. I have some research papers on the problem I can forward to you and I'm happy to look at the biopsy results. Not that I want to push myself on this institute."

"I, for one, would love the outside opinion," she said. "I'm such a novice and this sheep is my responsibility at the moment." She leaned in as the light caught the ewe's face just so—one bright eye clear and watchful, the other shadowed but open. "You definitely have something going on, Shambles." She reached out and put her hand on the animal's head.

"She's going to be just fine with the right treatment, Elise. I promise."

"Oh, there's the good news," she whispered to the sheep. "This handsome oncologist is going to fix you right up."

He chuckled. "Handsome?"

"Well, if she can't see real well at the moment..." Biting her lip, she squinted up at him. "I thought she should know the doctor's cute."

His mouth slid into a slow smile, then he leaned over and whispered into the sheep's ear. "Did you hear that, Shambles? She thinks I'm cute. Think she'll let me help with this Nativity thing? I'm kind of itching to get involved."

Her heart did a little dance, but she managed a casual shrug. "We might need an extra Wise Man."

"I can do gold, frankincense, myrrh, or penicillin. Just lead me to the manger."

She laughed, adoring his attitude. "Let's go out to the pen and meet the rest of the gang."

They stepped—or rather, rolled and walked—outside to the largest pen, where the stocky donkey watched and chewed, his ears flicking lazily.

Elise gestured. "That's Eeyore, our headliner who brings a very pregnant Mary into the stable. He knows his role is underappreciated."

"Not by Mary," he cracked.

The donkey brayed, earning a chuckle from Wade.

He crouched down near the fence, watching two

more goats nose each other for the best pile of hay. "They look happy."

"They are," she said softly. "It's kind of amazing, actually. No matter what they've been through, animals just—move on. They heal faster than we do."

"They do in the right hands," he said. "Which I can already tell you have."

"You can?" The compliment felt so good. "Thank you. But the real hero here is you, who figured out what was going on with that sheep's eye."

He gave a humble shrug. "Not that impressive when you consider I just finished years of oncology training. But taking on vet school, residency, and the big Christmas program? That's impressive."

Because she was in a wheelchair...or just because?

She didn't know and right that moment? She didn't care.

After checking all the animals, they wandered back out to the quad. The air outside had shifted, the clouds tinted pink and lavender against the snowy peaks.

They paused by a bench, where students were stringing white lights in the trees. Elise maneuvered her chair to face him as they sat in the fading sun, relaxed and enjoying the vibe. He gushed about his crush on Utah again, and showered compliments on the institute.

Finally, he leaned forward, elbows on his knees, and she braced herself for something...personal. She could see it in his eyes.

"I'm really grateful for Shambles," he said softly.

Oh. Shambles the sheep. That was a little disappointing. "Why?" she asked.

"She gave me the perfect excuse to come back here and see you."

And the rollercoaster she'd been riding all afternoon soared again. Biting her lip, she felt a flush deepen her cheeks, fighting the urge to ask him if he actually didn't notice she was in a wheelchair.

She swallowed that and gave a shaky smile. "You don't need an excuse."

His smile deepened, slow and genuine. "I'll take that as a good sign."

"A sign of...what?" she asked, almost afraid to hear the answer.

"That you like me as much as I like you." He winked at her.

"Are you *flirting* with me, Dr. Reynolds?"

"Not very well, if you have to ask."

"But..." She took a slow, deep breath, knowing that if they didn't talk about her disability, the conversation they never had would haunt her. "There is this small matter of an elephant."

"Yeah, yeah. The elephant in the room." He put one hand on each of her armrests and rolled her back two inches, then reversed to bring her even closer to him. "The one you think matters more than anything and would keep a guy from showing interest. That elephant?"

She nodded, unable to speak.

"I don't even see this alleged elephant," he said. "But I do see a striking, smart, funny, and insanely attractive woman who I'd really like to get to know better. I'm not begging to work on the Live Nativity because I have a hankerin' to spend Christmas Eve cleaning up sheep doo-doo."

"Then why are you?"

He slanted his head and gave her a look that said he couldn't believe she had to ask. But she had to ask! No one ever...no man had ever... Oh, dear.

She had to be honest. There was one other elephant in the room and he couldn't possibly know it. She had to tell him.

"I think you need to know something, Wade," she said on a rough whisper, forcing herself to get this out.

"Anything."

"I've never...been on a date. Never kissed a guy in my life. I don't know how to...do this. I've only watched movies and daydreamed and imagined...anything. I have no idea what I'm doing."

He just smiled. "No one does. That's what makes it fun. Can I see you again?"

She closed her eyes and sighed at his pure...goodness. "Yeah."

Lifting her hand, he pressed her knuckles to his lips. "Good. I'll text you. This was great. Thank you. Come on. Let's get you home, cowgirl."

He walked her back to the dorm, hugged her in the lobby, and gave her a kiss on the cheek. With a promise to call tomorrow, he left her with the biggest smile she'd worn in years.

This just didn't happen to Elise Hale.

But here it was...happening.

Chapter Seven
MJ

The dashboard clock read 10:14 a.m., but MJ's body felt battered and exhausted.

Because sleep had become the enemy.

Every night for darn near a week, she'd been jolted awake at exactly three a.m., her heart hammering, the same faint melody like a distant whisper, soft enough that she wasn't sure if she'd imagined it or not.

Then she'd get up, search, wait for it to stop, and cry, the notes of *What a Wonderful World* echoing maddeningly in her head. An ear *serpent*, not an earworm.

The second night, she decided she was overtired. The third, she was certain she'd lost the music box in her apartment and tore the place apart looking it. By the fourth, she was convinced George was sending her a message from heaven and, for some reason, he didn't want her to sleep.

Some reason named...Matt.

Glancing to her left, she took in Matt's strong profile behind the wheel of the Escalade he'd rented to navigate the winding mountain roads. Pines rose like sentinels behind snowbanks on either side of the canyons they cut through, sunlight glancing off branches so bright she had to squint.

"You okay over there?" Matt's voice was like honey, low and kind no matter what he said.

She blinked and forced a smile. "I'm fine. Really. Just didn't sleep much."

He glanced at her before turning back to the road. "That's the third day in a row you've said that. Are you feeling all right?"

The genuine concern touched her, a sign of a good man. Too good for her to confess that she thought her late husband was floating out from the heat vent in her apartment playing music so she would...not be in this car going to look at houses with that man.

"Did you find the music box you were looking for?"

She had told him about the lost box, but not why. And, once again, she chalked it up to class and goodness that he listened to her talk about something that might seem trivial to him.

"No," she said. "I looked everywhere. I just hope it didn't get bunched up in packing paper and accidentally thrown away."

"When was the last time you saw it?"

She grimaced because she absolutely couldn't remember, which was awful. Not only would she have lost a treasured memento, there'd be no explanation for the night music. None that wasn't...supernatural.

"I'm not sure," she admitted. "But I guess I'm just not sleeping well."

Matt waited as bit, then asked, "Is it this...errand? Is that what's troubling you, Mary Jane?"

Was it? Or was it the dear way he used her full name, which was not formal at all. On the contrary, it felt intimate and personal.

"Looking at houses for you to buy?" she asked, guessing that's what he meant by this errand. "I don't think I'm losing sleep over that."

Or was she?

"Are you sure?" he asked, the question echoing her doubts. "I would fully understand if this felt like too much. We talked about pacing this relationship and I want to do that."

That was true. He had promised that they would *take things slow*. No sudden moves, no sweeping declarations. Just quiet companionship and a lot of patience. He wasn't asking her to live in one of these houses...not yet, anyway.

She'd been grateful for that, but then that music woke her up every night.

"We're just fine," she assured him. "How many houses is it today? Three?"

"Three." He smiled. "A Goldilocks tour. Too cold, too hot, and maybe just right."

Just right for what, she wondered as she looked out the window. For him to live half an hour away from her and be her...boyfriend?

The word sounded preposterous at their age.

Would he eventually want her to live there, too? Of course, she wouldn't do that without the blessing of marriage and they certainly weren't at that point in this relationship.

But they could be…and then what? Did she want to leave the lodge? She loved her apartment! It was truly home, despite the recent torture.

"And she's thinking so hard again."

MJ laughed. "Sorry."

"Please, MJ." He reached over the console and took her hand. "Tell me what's on your mind."

"I did."

He squeezed her hand and slid a playful but easy-to-read look her way. "Come on, now. We're honest with each other, right? And open? Communication is key and all? So, tell me what's got you so quiet."

"Okay, okay." She sighed. "I'm wondering…what we are."

"What…like us? Our relationship? Is that what you mean?"

She nodded. "Are we…a couple?"

"A couple of what?" he joked, adding a wink. Then his expression grew serious. "Only if you want to be, MJ. This is all up to you."

"Me?" She nearly choked. "It takes two to be a couple."

"Well, I'm all in," he said without a second of hesitation.

All in? What did that mean? Even the word "couple" felt foreign to her. She'd never been a couple with anyone but George.

"Oh, looks like we're here," he said, glancing at the

dashboard screen and saving her from deepening the conversation. "Pick this up later? Over dinner?"

She nodded, looking out the window as the house appeared around a bend—an architectural marvel of steel and stone perched on the edge of the canyon, all sharp lines and glass walls that caught the light like a prism.

"Now *this* is something," Matt said, pulling into the completely dry driveway—which meant it was heated.

MJ eyed the place doubtfully. "Wow, that's luxurious. I mean, if you like the spaceship-crashing-into-the-slopes concept."

He choked out a soft laugh and jutted his chin as the driver's door of a navy-blue Tesla opened and a tall man in his forties stepped out. "There's Christopher, my agent. Do you even want to see this place?"

She let out an unsteady breath, not sure how to answer that. Truthfully, as he'd said.

Gathering her thoughts, she turned to him. "I do want to see it, mostly out of curiosity. It's your house, Matt. My thoughts on it don't matter."

Disappointment clouded his eyes. "But I want you to like it. And I really value your opinion. And...I don't want to do this alone."

Do *what* alone? Buy the house or live in it? What was he asking her?

Christopher walked toward the Escalade, giving a wave and a warm smile. "Morning, Matt."

Matt held up his hand in greeting and turned to MJ, searching her face. "Let's just look and then we can talk, honey."

The endearment felt good, but she just nodded. They were here now, and she really was dying to see what a house like this looked like on the inside.

Climbing out, Matt handled the introductions and chatted with the Realtor, chummy enough that MJ realized these two knew each other fairly well. Matt had been in and out of the lodge frequently these last few days, but MJ had been preoccupied with the soft opening and a few new guests.

Obviously, Matt had been seriously house-hunting while she was making people comfortable.

With some small talk about the square footage, the HOA fees, and the asking price—all of which were quite high—they walked up to a massive contemporary front door and she followed Matt inside.

The entryway was like one for a small hotel, dazzling and open and ultra-modern. There was no furniture, as the owners had recently decided their ski house should be in Aspen instead of Park City.

"This was their second home," Christopher explained. "So it's essentially a blank slate for you to decorate."

Decorate? MJ looked around. Nothing she owned or would want to own would work in this soulless house.

"Come see the kitchen," Christopher said, gesturing for them to head to the back. "It's the heart of this house."

MJ looked around that heart—massive, icy, angular, and not even functional—and decided she simply couldn't cook here.

"You hate it," Matt murmured as Christopher stepped into the dining room to give them privacy.

"I'm not—"

"I know, MJ," he said. "But I do value your opinion."

She exhaled and looked around, taking in the panoramic window offering a mountain view that was probably half the reason the house cost so much. She took a few steps, hearing her shoes tap on floors that looked like an ice skating rink. Imagine walking barefoot across that marble, she mused. Imagine coming in on a snowy pre-dawn to make tea in this...mausoleum.

Horrifying.

"It, um, doesn't have a heart," she replied as he watched and waited.

"Yeah, it's...sterile," he agreed.

They exchanged a few looks of mutual distaste as Christopher walked them through the rooms and pointed out the many luxurious features.

He was obviously good enough at his job that he picked up on their opinion, even though they didn't say a thing. Before he even opened the door that led to the walk-out basement and media room, he tapped his electronic tablet.

"On to the next?" he asked. "I think it might be more to your liking."

A few minutes later, they were back in the SUV, with the GPS programmed for house number two. MJ shifted in her seat, suddenly wondering why the questions about living in the same town or being in a relationship hadn't plagued her for the last year. She'd just hoped Matt would return and knew they had great potential to be...a couple.

There was that word again.

"Want to talk about something completely different?" Matt asked.

"You do know me pretty well," MJ replied, laughing.

"I know you're figuring things out, and I promised you space and time to do that. So, let me tell you about Wade's visit to that vet college that Elise attends."

"Oh? He went to Great Basin?"

"He did and came back quite enthused."

"About the school or..."

"About everything," he said. "He absolutely loves Utah and never expected to. He was blown away by the school, which is apparently quite unique in the veterinary world, and he is, uh...smitten."

"With Elise?" Her voice rose with a little thrill. "Oh, how nice. Elise is a beautiful young woman who is absolutely not defined by her disability. I'd love to see her find someone."

He reached over for her hand. "Listen, today is just an exploratory and fun trip to see houses. I do have to live somewhere. This is just...an option. Don't worry."

"I'm not worried," she said, but even as the words came out, she knew they weren't entirely true. "Tell me more about Wade and Elise."

He didn't have much to add and MJ made a mental note to get the details from Nicole, but was happy for the change of subject. Holding his hand, she watched the gorgeous scenery pass as they made their way to the next showing, joking about how they could be on *House Hunters*.

The second house sat lower in the valley, a weathered cedar-sided home that had once been grand and massive but now felt extremely dated.

"The eighties called and wants their sunken living room back," Matt joked softly as they walked into the front of the house and eyed a double curved staircase.

Still, the place had...warmth. MJ stood in the entry and let the faint scent of pine resin and history hit her.

"Oh," she whispered. "This place has stories."

Matt looked around at the dated wallpaper and dusty built-ins. "This place has potential."

"This place has termites," Christopher corrected gently. "But the lot is spectacular and the seller is motivated."

MJ drifted through the living room, fingers tracing a scarred banister. She imagined Christmases here—but not *her* Christmas. That would have to be at Snowberry Lodge forever and ever.

This house could make someone happy. Just not... her.

She gasped when she reached the two-story great room. Everything else fell away at the sight of an unobstructed 180-degree view of mountains, canyons, and the shockingly beautiful blue water of the Jordanelle Reservoir. The entire vista looked like a Swiss Alps lake that would never, ever get old.

"Oh, wow!" She pressed her hands to her chest. "I've

never seen that water from this high in the mountains. It's unbelievable."

"That's the money shot," Christopher said, stepping next to her. "This house will be gutted and renovated, quadruple in value, and always offer that million-dollar view. You'd just have to do a massive reno, Matt."

Matt and MJ shared a look and she shrugged. "Count on a year of hell, dirt, money, setbacks, and problems. But in the end, you might love it."

He made a face like he wasn't interested in that. "Yeah, you buy the view. And it's far," he added. "From Snowberry."

Which would matter if they were...a couple.

They spent half an hour exploring before conceding the house would require a fortune and several miracles. Back in the car, Matt grinned at her. "One more. Can you stand it?"

"I can," she said, her never-ending well of optimism apparently full again. "This is fun."

"That's what I wanted to hear," he exclaimed, taking her hand in a move that was now...the only way he drove.

She didn't hate that, either.

The final house sat at the end of a quiet cul-de-sac, framed by evergreens. Christopher hadn't seen this one yet, but he said the owner was a musician and songwriter, and the pictures looked great.

A wide porch wrapped around the front, its railings strung with white lights that glowed even in daylight. The style was a blend—stone foundation, timber beams, sleek glass doors. Modern, yet warm. When MJ stepped inside, her breath caught.

It *felt* right. Cozy but open, sunlight pouring through the windows, fireplaces on both floors. The kitchen was a dream—farmhouse sink, deep counters, a massive pantry.

Matt leaned on the island, eyes twinkling. "I can picture you in here."

She turned. "Me? You mean...you."

He shrugged. "I like this place and if I lived here, I'd want you to—"

"You have to see the downstairs." Christopher joined them from an open stairwell that led to the basement. "It's insane."

Grateful for the interruption, she turned and walked to the steps.

For whatever reason, Matt stayed in the kitchen while she walked down the carpeted stairs to a rambling walk-out basement. There was plenty of light and space, with the same cozy woodwork and layout that made this house feel wonderful.

On the far side, she pushed open a door to an unexpected theater room, with two rows of leather recliners, a huge screen, and music, movie, and TV posters framed on the walls.

Completely alone, she took a deep breath and tried to imagine...living here with Matt. She tried to picture coming home from the lodge after work, making dinner in that beautiful kitchen, cozying up in here to watch a fun movie.

It would be...not lonely. Nice, even. It might actually be amazing.

The images of a life together bounced around her head, and every one of them managed to be appealing and terrifying at the same time.

Wasn't this better than a quiet, secluded apartment above Snowberry? She wasn't sure.

"Could I trade that for this?" she whispered, turning to take another look around.

As she did, she spotted a glass door that led to one more room. Windowless and off to the side, she pushed open the door to a very dark room with...padded walls?

Reaching for a light switch, she bathed the room in the softest amber light, and realized it was for producing music, with guitars, a keyboard, and a set of drums.

Remembering the owner was a musician, she started to back out of the tiny space when her gaze caught on the wall covered with framed record jackets —all vintage and iconic. Elvis Presley. Frank Sinatra. Billie Holiday.

At the far end, spotlighted above a leather sofa, hung a black-and-white photograph of Louis Armstrong, trumpet poised mid-note. Beside it, the familiar record sleeve: *What a Wonderful World.*

Her pulse stuttered.

"Oh," she whispered.

Matt came up behind her, startling her. "Oh, look at this gem of a space."

"I think the owner uses this as a recording studio," Christopher said, appearing in the doorway.

MJ looked from one man to the other, literally unable to speak.

All she could hear was the faint ghost of that melody threading through her head again—the same one that had awakened her night after night.

It was as if the universe had tilted. Every hair on her arms stood on end.

"MJ?" Matt's voice was gentle. "You okay?"

She nodded too quickly. "Fine. Just...it's cold down here."

"You sure? You look like you've seen a ghost."

I have, she thought.

She backed toward the stairs. "Maybe we should—uh —head up."

By the time they reached the living room, her pulse had steadied, but her heart hadn't. Christopher waited by the front door, expectant.

"So," he said cheerfully, "what do you think?"

MJ opened her mouth, then closed it. She couldn't form the words.

Matt looked at her, reading everything she wasn't saying. His jaw tightened slightly, but when he turned to the Realtor, his voice was calm. "It's not quite right for *us.*"

Us. The word landed like a pebble in her chest, rippling outward.

Christopher nodded, unfazed. "Fair enough. I'll keep an eye out for others."

Outside, the light was fading to that pink-gold. Snowflakes drifted lazily, catching in MJ's hair as she climbed into the passenger seat. They sat in silence until Matt started the engine. Soft jazz filled the cabin—something instrumental and low.

"I'm sorry," he said finally.

"For what?"

"For...whatever that was back there that upset you. For pushing you on this errand. For not keeping my promise about taking things slow."

"You don't owe me an apology, Matt. I'm just still..." Grieving? Missing my husband? Unsure? "Getting used to the idea of an...us. I know it's been a year, but it all feels like it's happening too soon."

It was the best she could do without admitting that she was hearing—and now seeing—reminders of her late husband and she was sure he was telling her...not to pursue this.

"You set the pace, MJ," he said. "I promised that and I meant that."

The sincerity in his tone made her throat ache. "It's not you," she whispered. "It's just... complicated."

"I know," he said softly, starting the SUV. "I'm not here to upend your life. Just make it better."

Her eyes stung again. Outside, the mountains blurred in the dusk. She thought about that basement, the photograph, the song. Was it a coincidence? Or a warning? She didn't know which scared her more—the possibility that George was still guiding her, or that he wasn't.

They drove the rest of the way in quiet, headlights cutting through the gathering snow. When the lodge finally came into view—its windows glowing, wreaths on every door—MJ felt both relieved and heartsick.

Matt parked and turned to her. "Dinner later? Or do you need time to think?"

"I need time with you," she answered, her heart mellowing as she looked at him. "So, yes. Let's have dinner."

He leaned in, brushed a light kiss to her temple and then turned off the engine and got out, circling to open her door like the gentleman he was.

As she stepped onto the snow-packed drive, she lifted her eyes to the darkening sky. Snowflakes danced in the porch lights like confetti from heaven. For one dizzy instant she could almost hear George's chuckle, that warm baritone she'd loved all her life.

What was he trying to tell her? She couldn't give any hope to Matt until she figured that out.

Chapter Eight

Gracie had never expected tonight to feel this... right.

The original plan had been a sweet, grown-up sort of evening when she and Marshall would decorate his tree together while sipping wine, listening to classic Christmas carols, maybe sharing a kiss under a string of lights. A *holi-date,* as he'd so cleverly named it.

But plans changed, and Gracie was not mad about that.

Bianca had suddenly announced she had a mysterious errand in town and couldn't take Olivia, which probably meant she was Christmas shopping. Olivia had jumped on the opportunity to stay with her dad instead of alone at the Snowberry Lodge cabin.

When Marshall relayed that to Gracie, apologizing that it changed the vibe of their holi-date, she suggested that she bring Benny and they make a pizza night of decorating the tree. Of course, everyone was happy.

To be honest, the idea of the four of them decorating that tree together made her just as warm inside as the thought of being alone with Marshall.

Maybe even a little more because it felt so natural

and the kids were utterly hilarious in their approach to tree decorating. With Benny and Olivia, ornament placement was somehow a science, an art, and a challenge—and those two never backed down from any of those things.

So here she was, standing in Marshall Hampton's living room with the fire crackling, a beautiful evergreen standing near the window, and two kids giddy with sugar-fueled excitement—Marshall had caved on the cookies she brought.

Newt lay sprawled dramatically beneath the lowest branches, apparently confident that everyone needed his furry moral support. Kat sat primly beside him, tail wrapped around her paws like a Victorian governess ready to supervise the children's behavior.

The whole evening, from arrival through pizza to the opening of the ornament boxes, Gracie could feel her massive crush slowly take baby steps toward something far more significant.

"Tinsel?" Benny pulled out a bag of wavy silver threads. "This is so retro."

"That was my mother's, as many of the ornaments are," Marshall told him. "We put the tinsel on one strand at a time at the end or you'll hear the wrath of Germaine in your sleep tonight."

Olivia snorted. "Wrath? She'd smother you with hugs and kisses."

Benny put the tinsel down, either not willing to risk that or not interested in something that took that long. Then he snapped open another box of ornaments.

"Do we have a plan?" he asked.

"A plan?" Gracie blinked.

"A decorating plan," Benny explained. "Color coordination, size and scale, quality in front, junky school art in the back."

"Hey, I like the school art," Marshall said.

"Of course we have a plan," Olivia replied, sounding a little put out that he'd even ask. "Alternate colors, don't put the same too close to each other, put the best ones in the front, and I will hang the tinsel one at a time because my Grammy G showed me how."

"Perfect," Benny said, clearly happy with that plan. "Should we draw a diagram to follow?"

"Oh, Benny!" Olivia exclaimed. "Even I don't need a diagram for this."

"Just don't drop an ornament, Benny," Gracie reminded him.

Marshall came up beside Gracie, leaning close enough to whisper, "They're not all heirlooms, I promise. And anyone who has a plan does not break an ornament." He brushed her hand with his. Just a tiny touch. Just enough to make her stomach do a quick flip. "You want an adult beverage while there are still a few hours before you have to drive home?"

She didn't need anything to make her any more light-headed than the man in front of her. "I'm good with my apple cider, but thank you."

Marshall's eyes softened. "Then let me try it this way...there's a kitchen emergency."

She frowned. "What's wrong?"

"Too many kids and dogs," he murmured, tugging her gently, "so I need you alone for a moment."

Laughing at how completely unsubtle he was, she slipped away with him to the kitchen, which was warm and lit by the under-cabinet glow. On the island were the remnants of their empty pizza box and scattered paper plates that had been abandoned for the fun of tree decorating.

As soon as they were alone, Marshall pulled Gracie close and kissed her.

"Oh..." She whispered against his lips. "That wasn't in...the plan."

"Yes it was." He chuckled and kissed her again. "Then my plans for alone time morphed into a family night."

Drawing back, she searched his face. "I don't actually mind it—"

"I love it," he said. "But I didn't want to forget that tonight was supposed to be a date."

"Rain check?"

"As many as you want." Once again, he leaned down and kissed her, this time not rushed at all but full of affection and connection.

When he lifted his head, she sighed into him.

He brushed his thumb along her cheek. "You know, I thought tonight would be the two of us with wine but..." He glanced toward the muffled sounds of giggling from the living room, "somehow this is just as perfect. Maybe more."

She nodded. "Yeah. It really is. Those two are so easy and fun. And smart."

"The kids are good, too," he cracked, making her laugh. As her smile faded, he slid a warm hand under her hair, holding her head in his large palm. "I just had to bring you back here to tell you something."

She lifted her brows, waiting and wondering. Also melting into his arms.

"I'm crazy about you," he whispered. "I really think this could be something lasting and real."

Her breath caught. "Marshall…"

He kissed her lightly. "Not pushing. Just telling you the truth."

She rested her forehead against his. "I like the truth."

Before she could say anything else, Olivia shouted from the other room:

"Dad! Benny's trying to hang the glitter snowflake upside down!"

"Not upside down!" Benny yelled. "Artistic!"

Marshall groaned. "We should go rescue the tree."

"Probably."

They stepped back into the living room to see headlights pulling into the driveway.

"You expecting someone?" Gracie asked, but even as she said the words, she had a bad feeling about who this could be.

He just shook his head and walked to the door, leaving her in the living room with the kids, waiting for—

"Bianca."

Waiting for *that*.

A second later, Bianca swept into the living room in a whirl of cold air, high heels, the scent of expensive perfume, and enough attitude to freeze the fireplace.

"Oh...you're all here," she said, her dark eyes sweeping over Benny and Gracie. "Well, good, you can be my witnesses, since you're so connected to that lodge."

"Connected?" Gracie scoffed. "My mother and aunt run it and I'll no doubt inherit it someday. Is something wrong?"

Bianca's eyes shuttered as she seemed to consider how to respond. "Under the circumstances, I should tell you this alone, Marsh."

"You can tell me here," he said calmly, clearly well versed in Bianca's dramatics. "Anything."

"I need to be alone with you," she practically whined.

Just then, Gracie noticed the car lights leaving, which meant Bianca had come by Uber and wasn't going anywhere. *Dang it.* The warm bubble of their night popped so fast Gracie almost felt the temperature drop.

Newt barked once, then trotted over to sniff the newcomer's boots suspiciously. Kat, sensing drama, leapt onto the back of the sofa like she needed the high ground.

Marshall froze, eyebrows lifting with curiosity. "Bianca? What's going on?"

Bianca pressed a shaking hand to her chest. "There was—there was a thing in my cabin."

"What kind of thing?" Olivia asked.

Bianca shuddered dramatically. "A spider. A monstrous spider. Practically prehistoric. The thing was the size of a dinner plate, I swear on my life."

Benny's mouth twitched. Gracie shot her son a look that said: *not one word.*

Her genius son was surely thinking what she, born and raised in Utah, already knew. Wolf spiders—a creature that barely broke a few inches and could never be described as the size of a dinner plate—would be deeply burrowed underground in December. Not even the heat of a fire could coax them out of their warm winter holes.

"It was directly over my bed!" she exclaimed when no one seemed to be upset enough to suit her.

"Did you call my mother?" Gracie asked. "MJ is on-site in the lodge and she'd have come kill it for you."

"I asked for help," she continued, sounding purposely vague, "and no one came! I could've died, because that thing *had* to be poisonous. Now I'm shaking all over and I just... I can't go back. I need to stay here tonight."

Marshall blinked. "Here?"

"Where else would I stay?" She glanced at the tree and the kids. "I didn't know this was a family tree decorating night."

When four unsmiling faces looked at her, she threw off her coat. "Well, I know how this goes," she announced. "The silver hairy stuff goes one at a time, right? Your mother was the original control freak who wouldn't let us toss the tinsel."

She looked from one to another, no doubt seeing Olivia's dismay, Marshall's disgust, Benny's curiosity, and Gracie's ache for this woman to leave as quickly and unexpectedly as she'd arrived.

"Don't get comfortable." Marshall crossed his arms. "You cannot stay here."

"Well, I can't stay there with a spider the size of that tree spinning a web over my head. He could fall in my mouth!"

Benny snorted, earning a vile look from Bianca.

"Benny," Gracie whispered, gesturing to him. "Maybe we should give them some privacy."

"Not necessary," Marshall said, putting a very possessive arm around her. "We don't need privacy and we sure don't need help. Call the Uber back, Bianca. You're not staying here."

Bianca's expression sharpened. "Marshall. Please."

He didn't budge.

And Gracie, watching him stand his ground—with kindness, not anger—felt something unfurl warm and proud inside her.

Bianca's face pinched as she realized she wasn't winning. "Fine. Then you're coming with me, Olivia. Let's go." She whipped her coat off the sofa and pulled it back on. "We'll wait outside in the cold for our car."

"Bianca."

"Mom!"

She fished for her phone, somewhere in the bowels of a designer bag. "Get your things, honey. We need to leave. Now."

Olivia looked torn, wide-eyed, and so uncomfortable.

"What?" Bianca snapped, loud enough that both dogs sat up, alert. "This is my holiday with you. You're in my custody and shouldn't even be here. I'm taking you home and I don't want an argument. And you"—she pointed at Marshall—"can't stop me."

"Not legally," he said. "But is this really what you want to do?"

"No," she shot back. "I want to sleep here, safe and spider-free."

Gracie expected him to cave, but Marshall stood his ground, shaking his head.

"Mom, I don't want to go! Dad, please don't make me. This is fun."

Marshall let out a noisy sigh. "Sweetheart, it's okay. We'll finish the tree tomorrow. You go with your mom."

Olivia grunted, obviously not getting what she wanted.

Then Benny straightened up, puffing out his chest. "I'll come, too."

Gracie blinked. "You will?"

"Yeah. I'm, like, the best spider-finder in Utah. I can totally clear the cabin and maybe Olivia can come back after."

"I think it'll be too late, honey," Gracie said.

"Well, that's fine," Benny replied. "I can kill a spider with my eyes closed."

Gracie's heart softened at her son's earnest bravery and willingness to leave with Olivia. "Sweetie, that's really kind of you."

Bianca glared, then looked at her phone. "Well, the Uber can't be here for forty minutes, so—"

"So I'll drive you and the kids back to the Lodge," Gracie offered automatically.

"No," Marshall said immediately, pulling out his own phone. "You're staying. And on my app? The ride can be here in...four minutes. Probably the guy who just left."

Bianca's shoulders dropped, defeated. "Fine. Do I have time to use the bathroom or is that off-limits, too?"

"Help yourself," he said, tapping his screen.

"Don't order the ride," Gracie said when Bianca stepped away. He looked up with a question in his eyes, but she shook her head. "I'll drive everyone home."

"No!" Olivia said. "I really wanted to finish the tree with you."

"We will," Gracie promised. "Tomorrow."

"But I like tonight." Olivia's voice dropped so Bianca couldn't hear. "Us being together. Like a...team."

Gracie's throat thickened. "Me, too."

"Please, Dad. Tell her to take the Uber back and we can stay."

He shook his head, looking as sad as his daughter. "She has legal rights and I can't insist she leave you here."

"Then I have to sleep in the room with the spider?"

Benny choked. "There are no spiders in the winter in Utah. I mean, it would be rare."

"So she's making it up," Olivia said, and it wasn't question.

"If she is, you're fine," Benny said. "If she isn't, I will find it and take it outside to a nice burrow hole where it belongs at this time of year."

Gracie's heart folded in half as she leaned over and kissed her son on the head. "Proud of you, Benny."

Marshall reached out to him, too. "You're a good man, Ben. I like someone who has sense in a crisis."

"I have sense!" Olivia exclaimed with a pout.

"And so do I," Gracie said. "I don't want them in an Uber. Let me drive us all home."

Marshall huffed a frustrated breath. "Okay, Gracie. But can you come in the kitchen with me for a moment?"

Once again, they walked back to the privacy of his chef's kitchen, but this time it didn't feel romantic and secret. Just...sad.

Marshall rubbed the back of his neck and finally looked at her with that same soft, private smile.

"Well," he murmured, "that happened."

Gracie laughed. "It certainly did."

"She's a drama queen who wants something from me," he said. "That's a bad combination."

"What do you think she wants?"

"A second chance." He held up a hand at Gracie's wide-eyed reaction. "Don't worry, that isn't happening. But I don't like to antagonize her because I worry about her influence on Olivia."

"I get that," Gracie said. "And it makes me happy that Benny's father is out of the picture and wants to stay that way."

"I thought Bianca was, too, but something changed." He stepped closer. "Sorry the night blew up like this."

"No apologies necessary. We'll finish the tree tomorrow or whenever we can. Lots of Christmas ahead."

He closed the distance, reaching out to her. "True. Silver lining." He folded her in an embrace, drawing her into his chest, closing every inch of space between them. "But this felt like...a glimpse."

Her breath caught. "A glimpse?"

He took her face gently in his hands. "Of what could be." He kissed her softly, tenderly, like he'd been thinking about it for a while and really had to get it right.

As for Gracie, she now knew the actual meaning of the word swoon. With a little dizziness thrown in.

While her eyes were closed, he kissed her deeper, this time slow and certain, his hands threading into her hair.

When they finally broke apart, foreheads touching, breath mingling, she whispered, "I like that glimpse. I like it a lot."

"Good," he said.

"I'm ready!" Bianca announced, her boot heels knocking on the floor as she approached the kitchen.

Gracie started to jerk out of his arms, but Marshall held her tight, as if he refused to hide their relationship.

Bianca stood in the doorway and sliced Gracie with a withering glare. "It's snowing. Does that bakery van handle the snow?"

"You better hope so," Gracie quipped, sliding out of Marshall's arms and catching the flicker of amusement in his eyes.

A few minutes later, the bakery van rolled away. In the back with the dogs, Benny and Olivia sat quietly, both looking a bit disappointed.

Bianca took out her phone and never looked up or spoke to them.

So Gracie put on some cheesy Christmas music and

tried not to sing, smile, or share the fact that she was, indeed, falling head over heels for Marshall Hampton.

Chapter Nine

How in the name of all that was holy did he end up taking a hike across all twenty-five acres of Snowberry Lodge and beyond? Red Starling didn't *hike*.

He also didn't chat about macros—whatever the heck they were—or care about bone density and something called his "mitochondrial" health or, God help him, lymphatic drainage.

Yet somehow, someway, that's what he got roped into today by Bertie Kessler, an unstoppable force of nature who refused to take no for an answer. Once again, she'd snagged him as he'd made his way from the lodge up to the house, a long nap in his future.

Now, he was marching in the snow listening to a very talkative old workhorse yammer about the "pillars of health" like they were the second coming.

"Come on, now, Red. Let's get to your house. What is that? Half a mile, uphill?"

He moaned because it was easier than talking.

"Hard things make strong people." Bertie grinned up at him, her blue eyes bright behind bifocals. "You want to be strong, don't you, Red?"

"I want to be drinking something hot in front of the fire," he muttered. "With my crossword puzzle."

"Oh, that's fantastic for your brain," she said, tugging on that ridiculous giant fur hat. "Gotta stay alert and sharp or we get old."

"Must be, 'cause I live for that puzzle." Although, right now, he felt like he might die trying to get to it.

"Not good, not good," she said, making him slow his step.

"What's not good?" he demanded. "You just said it was fantastic."

"Did you not listen to my speech about the pillars of health?"

Not a word, he thought.

"Of course you didn't," she said. "Nutrition, movement, sleep, and purpose!" She slathered all kinds of emphasis on the last one. "You must have a *purpose*. We're too old for jobs, so we need to have something that matters."

"The *New York Times* crossword puzzle matters," he said, knowing it sounded like a weak argument, probably because it was. Or maybe because this last hill was murder.

"It doesn't really matter because it's inanimate," she explained. "You need a soul involved. A person, a pet, a hobby that improves people's lives. My purpose is helping old folks realize their physical potential."

"Or killing them," he said under her breath.

"One more corner, Red," she prodded. "And while you do it, tell me your purpose."

He tried to think of something that would shut her up, but he went blank.

"Come on, what matters to you every day?" she pressed. "What brings you joy, comfort, and a reason for waking up in the morning?"

Would she accept biscotti? Probably not.

"You better give me an answer or we're doing another mile."

He slid her a dark look. "Fine. I like...naps. There's nothing better, 'cept maybe my granddaughter's baking, that crossword puzzle, another nap, possibly a good game of Monopoly with Benny and a plate of cookies." He grinned at her. "Followed by a nap. You see a pattern there?"

To her credit, she laughed heartily. Maybe there was a beating heart in that drill sergeant's body. "Well, the answer was buried in there," she said. "Benny. He's your purpose."

The words hit harder than he expected—unless that was his heart on the verge of a full-blown attack.

"Yeah, he's very important to me."

"How?"

He rolled his eyes like he did every time she threw in a little therapy with her miserable exercise.

"I'm the only man in his life," he said, the answer popping into a head that had obviously been cleared of rational thought from all this walking.

"My son Jack is around," she fired back.

He nodded. "He is, but he's Cindy's husband, running the lodge, and doing sleigh rides. He's not a constant in Benny's life. I live with the kid and his mother and we're...tight." He smiled and this time it was genuine. "He says I'm his best friend, although that sweet little Olivia might have dethroned me."

She considered that, nodding. "That's a lot of responsibility, Red." Her voice was serious, and so were the words. "What happens to Benny if you die?"

He stopped mid-march, opening his mouth to make a typical Red Starling quip. But none came out. Instead, he looked at her, but in his head, all he could see was Benny-bean's sweet face and how it had crumpled the day he thought Red was having a heart attack on the ice.

"He'd be in trouble," Red admitted.

"Then your purpose is making sure he's taken care of when you're gone."

"Well, he can have whatever money I've got, he can live in the house that Starlings have been in for generations, and his mother will never abandon him."

"But who will be the *man* in his life?" she asked. "Who will be his role model? Who will teach him how to tie a bowtie or fix a carburetor or what to say on his first date?"

They reached the snow-covered lawn of the old house at the edge of the property as Red contemplated the questions...and hated the answer. Benny's first date would be in five or six years, likely. Red would be kissing ninety. If he made it.

"I don't know," he finally admitted. "I hate to say this because it will just encourage you, but I guess my purpose is to make sure I don't die."

"Oh, you will," she deadpanned. "I think your purpose is to make sure Benny has someone in his life when you do."

How would he do that? He just stared at her, wishing she was wrong but knowing she wasn't.

Then she pulled the fur beast on her head even lower. "Enjoy your nap! I've got two more miles and then I'm going to have a healthy and nutritious meal with the nice balance of macros. You remember what they are, right?"

"Sugar, fat, and beer?" he joked.

Again, she surprised him by giving a belly laugh and taking off down the path, leaving him catching his breath and thinking about their conversation.

How could he make sure Benny had someone in his life? He could start by not dying...and the only way he knew to do that was to take a nap.

So he went inside, kicked off his boots, slid out of his jacket, and hit the recliner. But he couldn't even nap. All he did was think about Benny—his best friend, his great-grandson, his purpose.

"GRANDPA! Wake up! I have to talk to you!"

Okay, maybe he'd napped after all.

Red cracked one eye, no stranger to the sight in front of him. His great-grandson stood over him, eyes wide behind his always slightly crooked glasses, hair sticking up in six different directions, breathing like he'd just done a marathon with Bertie the Beast.

"Are you bleeding? Is there a fire? Are we under an avalanche warning?" Red opened the other eye and tugged the afghan up to his chin. "If not, leave a message and I'll call back later."

"It's worse," Benny said. "It's Olivia's mom...the Bianca lady."

The Bianca *lady*? Hardly. More like the harlot who wanted to ruin Marshall Hampton's life.

"Bianca," he repeated, his voice gravelly as he dragged himself out of the nap. "What's she doing now?"

"Ruining everything, Grandpa. *Everything!*"

Red slowly lifted the recliner lever, groaning as the chair back straightened and his complained. "Start from the top, Benny-bean."

"She just wants to wreck everything," Benny declared, throwing his arms in the air. "She destroyed our tree decorating last night and then I had to go in the cabin and look for a spider that wasn't ever there and while I was, she told Olivia that Mom can't go over to Marshall's house anymore."

"What?"

"And today, Olivia told me her mom might move here. *To Park City!*"

Red rubbed his face. He should've known this nap was doomed. "You sure she said all that?"

"Yes! She said she and Marshall 'deserve a second chance.'" Benny made air quotes so exaggerated he nearly lost his balance. "You know what that means, don't you? She's gonna try to *steal* him from my mother."

Red winced at the crack in Benny's voice, matching the one he could feel in his heart.

Bianca wasn't just here to play house. No, siree. She was here to snare a good man in a bad way.

The memory of overhearing—*maybe*—her evil plans made his stomach turn. He had yet to tell a soul, hoping the problem would solve itself without Red having to stick his nose where it didn't belong.

Apparently, that wasn't going to happen.

"So we gotta do something," Benny insisted, plopping into the chair across from him. "We can't just let her stay here and wreck everything."

Red scratched his chin, knowing the "something" to do was alert Marshall. Or Gracie. Or someone who would put a stop to this, but the very idea made him a little ill. It wasn't his business and he shouldn't act on something he wasn't even sure he heard while he was hiding out in her cabin like a serial killer.

Who would even believe him?

"But I have a plan," Benny said, his eyes fiery with a mission. "You want to hear it?"

Did he? Probably not. "Hit me," Red said.

"We make her hate it here so bad she wants to leave."

Red snorted, no stranger to Benny's wild and frequently dangerous ideas. "Think we can irritate her right out of the state?"

"Maybe. I got some clues last night about what might really freak her out."

Red tilted his head. "Freak her out?" He certainly didn't want to break a pregnant woman, just get her to ditch her dumb schemes. "What are you thinking, Benny?"

"Wildlife," Benny said, utterly serious. "That lady is terrified of anything that walks, breathes, and lives in the woods."

"So...you want to scare her away."

"It could work," he said. "Maybe something like... snow snakes."

"Snow what now?"

Benny's eyes lit up. "We tell her that there are these rare winter snakes that slither under the powder. Totally harmless—but super gross. Then we sprinkle, like, garden hoses or something around her cabin at night so she flips out when she opens the door."

Red stared, hating that the idea had merit, but that woman was too smart for that. Also, maybe pregnant, and he just didn't want her getting hurt. "Do better," he said, and Benny—bless his heart—nodded.

"Raccoons?" he suggested without hesitation. "We could wrangle some to knock garbage cans around outside her cabin."

Red gave him a withering look. "Wrangle raccoons? Good luck with that."

"Okay, okay." He snapped his fingers, thinking, undaunted. "How about a baby bear? Opossum? Maybe just a standard rat that gets into her cabin."

Red choked. "A rat? Benny! The woman is pr— problematic."

"You're right. She'll sue Snowberry Lodge for all we've got." Benny mussed his mop of hair as he ran his fingers through it, as though he could rub that amazing brain into a higher gear. "We need something scary but not...real."

Or maybe Red could confront the woman and shame her into leaving?

Benny practically leaped in the air, giving a clap with a soft hoot. "I got it, Grandpa! I totally know how to scare her away with something that isn't real but she couldn't handle."

"What?"

Benny beamed, put his hands on his hips, and narrowed his gaze behind his angled glasses. "Bigfoot."

Red snorted so hard he needed a tissue. "Bigfoot?"

Benny nodded, dead serious. "I've been watching videos."

"Exactly why you shouldn't have a phone."

"Seriously, Grandpa. People *swear* he lives out here and they call him...the Wasatch Sasquatch!"

"That's a mouthful."

Benny jumped again. "But Bigfoot is scarier. So we make her think he's real and he's hanging around her cabin."

Red pressed his lips together, fighting the grin creeping up. "You plan to dress up like...Bigfoot?"

"I was thinking more just... sound-effects. And some footprints in the snow. Maybe a big hairy shadow in her window. We could—"

Red let out a belly laugh, cutting him off. "She's not

dumb, Benny. I could dress up as Santa and come down her chimney, too, and she wouldn't believe I was real. Bigfoot? Are you serious?"

"As a heart attack."

Red glared. "We don't make jokes about that," he said. "And this isn't a great idea."

"Well, what should we do?" Benny demanded.

Red knew exactly what to do—tell Marshall what he thought he'd overheard and let the man handle his own problems. Surely he'd boot his ex-wife's designer-clad behind out of here.

Or maybe he wouldn't. Maybe that softhearted former NFL player who loved the Lord would think he had to "do the right thing" and marry her. Maybe Marshall would believe that was best for Olivia, who was clearly the man's soft spot.

Maybe...Benny was right and they should just scare Bianca into leaving. Was Bigfoot the answer?

Of course not.

"Maybe something less extreme," Red said.

He sighed. "Okay, okay. We put some leftovers—like fish—outside her door tonight. That'll attract raccoons. They'll make a racket, she'll freak out, and—boom—she'll think the woods are dangerous."

"You realize raccoons carry rabies, right?" Red asked.

"Okay, no raccoons," Benny conceded. "Come on, Grandpa. A Bigfoot sighting is exactly what we need."

"No, a nap is what we need. And you just settle down and...do homework."

"School's out for winter break and...and...I'm scared, Grandpa."

"Of Bigfoot?"

"Of Bianca," he said, his voice heavy with sadness.

"You think she's going to stomp you with one of her high heels?"

Benny didn't laugh. His whole face fell into a serious scowl. "Marshall and Mom like each other," he said matter-of-factly. "They hold hands and whenever they think we're not looking, they kiss. And I like him, Grandpa. I want him to be around like...like..."

"Like a father?" Red suggested.

"I mean..." Benny swallowed. "Is it so bad to want that?'"

"No, Benny-bean. It's not bad at all." And Red, who currently held the status of father, grandfather, and great-grandfather to this wonderful little boy, had a responsibility to get that role filled just in case anything happened to him. "But no Bigfoot. I'm too old for your antics."

"I'm not."

"*Benny.*"

"Just kidding, Grandpa. Kind of. That woman is on a mission and she's exactly like Olivia when she wants something."

"Relentless," Red said.

"Yup. She never quits. Unless..." Benny grinned, the sight so good and innocent, it twisted Red's old heart. Good gravy, he loved this boy.

"Unless Bigfoot shows up," Red finished for him,

making Benny giggle. "The answer is no. No Bigfoot, no snow snakes, no raccoons, no antics."

Benny looked disappointed, but accepting. "'Kay. Then you can go back to sleep, Grandpa."

"Good call, Benny-bean." As he tugged at the blanket and Benny took off, Red settled back into his recliner, thinking about...his purpose.

His purpose was right here—keeping that boy safe, happy, and surrounded by good people who loved him. He just had to figure out how best to do that.

Chapter Ten

Elise

S hambles wasn't blinking. That was what worried Elise the most.

"Come on, girl," she murmured, resting her forearms on the top rail of the pen. The barn smelled like hay and animals and the faint metallic tang of the heat lamps. "You're supposed to be rehearsing for your big debut, not staring into space like a tragic poet."

The ewe stood with her head lowered, jaw making slow, distracted chews. The left eye, the good one, tracked Elise's voice. The right eye...didn't. The cloudy, angry-looking globe had always been unsettling, but ever since the biopsy, it felt like a countdown clock.

She reached through the rail and scratched the rough wool just behind the ewe's ear. "I got your results," she whispered. "It's exactly what that wonderful Dr. Reynolds thought."

Carcinoma. No more pretending it could be some weird irritation that would clear up with ointment and optimism.

"You are officially a medical case, my darling."

Shambles shifted her weight with a small snort, looking patently exhausted. Some of the other animals in the barn played and chewed on hay, but Shambles seemed dull around the edges, like someone had turned down her brightness.

Elise checked the time on her phone. Wade would be here any minute. They'd talked that morning—the first time she'd called him since he'd been here.

But not the first time they'd talked. The afternoon he left, they'd started—and kept—a running text conversation. He'd been waking her up with, "Good morning, cowgirl," and the exchange continued on and off during the day and ended late at night. They shared funny memes, told each other about their days, and kept a running chat that neither one seemed to want to end.

He also called her every evening, ostensibly to check on Shambles, and made a plan for him to come back after the biopsy results were in.

They hoped to celebrate, but...not this time.

She didn't like the lab report, but she sure did like Wade's instant reaction—he dropped plans he'd had with his uncle to make the hour-plus drive from Park City to Eagle Mountain to do what he could for Shambles.

She blew out a breath and nudged the sheep's muzzle.

"Would he come if you weren't sick?" she asked the animal in a breathy whisper. "Maybe. Probably. Who knows? I can't..." She leaned in to the sheep's curly fur. "I can't let my heart go there, Sham. I have to guard it. You understand that, right? I mean, I'm a girl in a wheelchair and he's...an unattainable dream."

She could only get hurt or disappointed, right? Yes,

he'd go back to Alabama after the holidays, and this would have been a nice interlude and maybe she'd get her first kiss, but she couldn't...

Then she remembered the look on his face when he revealed that he had known she was in a wheelchair and came to see her anyway. Every time she thought about that, she clung to hope.

A latch clinked near the front of the barn.

Her heart jumped at the same time her hands tightened on the wheel rims, pushing herself back to see who'd come in. She caught his silhouette in the barn door —tall, broad, masculine, delicious, and, oh, man—he was wearing that cowboy hat.

Not fair!

"Hey, there," Wade's voice called, easy and warm. "How's my girl?"

Her heart stuttered. "She's in pain, I think, but bearing up well."

He strode down the aisle of the barn, his face coming more in view with each step. He wore a pale blue denim shirt and jeans, the dark puffer vest, and that black hat that sent butterflies into flight from her throat to her belly.

When he reached her, he tipped back his hat, leaned down, and kissed her hair. "I meant the two-legged girl."

She looked up at him and had to swallow the quip that rose—"two legs that don't work"—because that was her old coping mechanism when attention was on her or her disability. She would always make a joke, mostly because it put other people at ease when they didn't know what to say.

But nothing needed to be said or done to put Wade Reynolds at ease. His steady demeanor was just another ridiculously attractive thing about him.

"Better now," she admitted with a soft laugh. "This isn't something I relish handling on my own and this place is a ghost town due to winter break."

"You're definitely not on your own," he assured her. "And neither is Miss Shambles." He turned and leaned against the half door of her pen, looking down at the sheep. "Heard you got some bad news, kiddo."

The way he spoke to the animal—like Shambles had a heart, soul, and spirit—knotted something tender in Elise's chest.

Elise reached into the side pocket of her chair to pull out her tablet to read the lab report.

"It says, "confirmed squamous cell carcinoma in the right eye,'" she read. "The margins on the sample were… not clean. Kudos on an impressive pre-test diagnosis."

He flicked his gaze from Shambles to her, all business now. "Can I see it? Did they give you a staging report or just the pathology?"

"Just pathology so far. I can pull it up if you want to see the exact wording." She tapped the screen. "But the bottom line is cancer." She swallowed. "As you know, Great Basin doesn't have an oncology department."

She hated how that last bit came out sounding like a failing on her part, like she should've somehow conjured one up.

Wade didn't look surprised. "It's a specialty practice and this institute is still growing," he said, opening the gate and walking into the pen. He snagged a stool that put him eye to eye with Shambles. "Some states only have one vet school that has oncology, especially out west where there's so much emphasis on large animals and livestock. Most of the time, oncology is just attached to a study for funding."

She wheeled in closer to the sheep, splitting her attention between Shambles and the way Wade moved into his examination.

He took off his cowboy hat and got close to Shambles, silent while he did an initial observation of the site.

Elise gave the ewe's wool a quick stroke. "I talked to Dr. Hayes—my professor—and she suggested calling in a local oncologist, but the farmer..." She exhaled. "He was very clear. He can't afford a specialist. He said he only offered Shambles for the Live Nativity because he thought it would be fun for his grandkids. He said he didn't know anything was wrong but he *had* noticed the eye was cloudy."

Wade's brows pulled together as he studied the sheep. "Did you explain the prognosis without treatment to him?"

"Yes. I told him the eye would get worse. That eventually it could ulcerate, become painful, maybe spread deeper. He asked me if she could see out of it now, and if she was in pain. I had to say not really. Maybe a little."

"She feels this," Wade said. "But it's not debilitating. Not yet, anyway."

"Well, his owner says Shambles is old, and he just doesn't have the money, especially right before Christmas."

Her voice cracked on the last word, which was mortifying. She cleared her throat and focused on some hay on the floor.

"I'm sorry," she said quietly. "I'm not usually this emotional about livestock cases. I know the realities. I know farmers can't always..." Her hands opened helplessly. "I just—he volunteered Shambles for a good cause. And I can't stand the idea of sending her back like this when there might be something we can do."

There was a small pause, then Wade turned to her. "Please don't ever apologize for caring. It's one of the most attractive things about you. One of many."

Her heart rolled around, flipped in the air, then took a dive to the hay-covered floor. "Thank you," she managed.

"What else did your professor say?" he asked as he pressed his thumb into the skin around the cancerous eye.

"She said if we wanted to pursue treatment, we'd have to run it through the teaching hospital like any other case. Which is closed for the semester, of course."

"Is there an emergency surgery or OR?"

She nodded. "Yes, but it's for true emergencies and I'm not sure this counts."

"To Shambles it does," he said.

"Of course, there's an expense involved and the school can't be responsible without a clear academic reason, and there's no current study that fits. The owner can't pay, Great Basin can't pay, and, technically, it's not an emergency *yet*. So it's kind of...stuck."

"Unless," he said, "someone with oncology training is willing to donate their time and the school provides space and tools for the procedure because it's teaching."

"Teaching?"

"Well, have you ever seen the excision of an ocular squamous cell carcinoma?"

"No."

"Then you'll be learning. And assisting. Surely there's extra credit for that."

She hardly dared to breathe. "Are you...offering that?"

"Yes." The answer was immediate. "If we can get into the emergency OR, the standard treatment is debulking with adjunct cryotherapy. It's not a complicated surgery, I promise. We'll just need the space, some equipment, light medication. We'll reduce the tumor load, clear her vision, lower the chance of recurrence, and get it done in an hour. The bulk of the expense is the specialist vet and..."

"And I'm looking at him."

"And I don't cost a thing." He tapped her nose playfully. "But rest assured because I got an A in my semester of ophthalmology and was number one in my soft tissue surgery class. Does that make you feel more confident in me?"

It made her feel dizzy with attraction. "I trust you," she said simply.

His smile flashed, quick and proud. "Good. Then how do we make it happen?"

"I'll plead the case to Dr. Choi, who is running the Emergency OR and Trauma Center over the holidays."

"Can you do that now?"

She nodded. "But we should remember that most of the faculty is out of town, and elective procedures are limited."

"Then you should make the case that this isn't elective," he said calmly. "We're preventing future pain, potential loss of the eye, and we're giving institute students a chance to observe a procedure they don't usually see here."

"Pretty sure you'll have a class of one."

He leaned closer. "Then you can be teacher's pet."

She took a sharp breath, a little overwhelmed by the impact of him. By his style and certainty, his warmth and compassion, and oh, those green eyes that ought to be illegal.

"You're not sure about this?" he asked, misreading what was probably an expression of complete and pathetic crush-ness.

"No, I am. I was just thinking..." *About kissing you.* "About how, uh, grateful I am for the help. I don't know how to thank you."

"You don't have to." His eyes softened. "I get to do what I love. You get experience. Shambles gets a shot at a merry little Christmas."

"Everybody wins," she said.

"Plus," he added, "I promised a certain veterinarianin-training that I'd help her with the Live Nativity. What is a Nativity scene without a sheep?"

"Exactly. Then I should try to get in to see Dr. Choi right now." She started to wheel back, but he turned and put a light hand on her arm.

"Would it be okay if I come with you?" he asked. "I can explain my training and credentials and put Dr. Choi in touch with someone from my school, too. I don't want to overstep, but..."

"Not overstepping at all," she assured him. "Thank you. I'd love the backup."

They gave Shambles a little love and a treat, then headed across campus together, laughing and talking the whole way like...well, not like friends.

Maybe that's what she was to him, but Elise couldn't deny that every minute she was with the guy, she wanted...more.

"Okay, I'm in love."

At Wade's admission, Elise's fingers gripped the thin metal roller and clicked the brakes—the wheelchair equivalent of stopping dead in her tracks. "Excuse me?"

"With this school," he said on a quick laugh, reaching down to put his hand on her shoulder as they left Dr. Choi's office and back into the sunshine. "I mean, we waited, what? Five minutes to get in to see an important member of the faculty. He listened to every word, read the report, went online and checked me out, and—wham —surgery is the day after tomorrow, assuming Shambles' owner agrees."

"And I do a paper on the treatment of ocular squamous cell carcinoma for next semester's class on large-animal disease." Elise grinned. "Now I don't have to think of a topic or do research. Win." She high-fived him.

"And Shambles will heal before the Live Nativity. I just never saw such efficiency."

"Well, Dr. Choi was blown away with your credentials, Wade. Third in your class? And you told me you won the American College of Veterinary Surgeons *fellowship* in surgical oncology. *Dude.*"

He chuckled. "They were diggin' in the bottom of the barrel."

"Stop it." She looked up, laughing and releasing her brake. "After graduating from Auburn's vet school and the oncology residence there, I can't imagine little old Great Basin is very impressive."

"Well, I'm impressed with this school, this state." He made a sweeping gesture toward the towering mountain range at the edge of the valley. "I sure didn't expect to feel this way."

"What did you expect? What made you come to Utah?"

"Truth? It was a favor to my mom."

"How so?"

"When my uncle finished his year of giving away mega-millions, I spent Thanksgiving with him at my parents' house," he explained. "He confessed that he'd met someone and they'd taken a shine to each other without her having any idea he'd won the lottery."

Elise smiled, knowing MJ's story with Matt through Nicole. "It's very romantic."

"Well, my mom, who is his younger sister, just wasn't so sure *how* romantic. No one knew anything about MJ. As far as timing, I'd just finished my residency and needed to clear my head before I start the whole process of deciding where I want to work. It made sense to do that out here and also make sure Uncle Graham, er, Matt, wasn't, you know..."

"Getting taken by a hustler like MJ," she finished when he didn't have a diplomatic way of saying that.

He laughed at the obvious sarcasm. "Pretty much. I've never been to Utah. I've been to California, flown over the Rockies, and went to a Veterinary Cancer Society regional conference in Billings, Montana, once. I thought I knew...the West." He slid a look at the mountains again, then back to her. "I had no idea that everything out here is insanely appealing. Now my uncle's looking at houses and I'm thinking..."

She swallowed, her whole body frozen.

"I could see joining him out here."

Her jaw dropped. "You're kidding."

He shrugged. "Not really. Open skies. Actual seasons. And not a lot of veterinary oncology, though I did find a few practices in Salt Lake City. There's a need."

There was a need, all right. In her heart.

"That's...wild." It was the best she could do. Because

if he stayed...she'd fall in love, dream of a life with him, and get wrecked when it didn't work out.

"Wild, but possible," he said. "What do you think of that?"

She drew back. "Me? I...I...yeah. Utah's amazing. The mountains and all the outdoor stuff, great people, very vibrant and growing, and...we have cute sheep."

He chuckled. "And vet students."

"Come for the sheep, stay for the students," she cracked, but when he didn't laugh, she glanced up and caught him looking hard at her, no smile on his face. "That was a joke," she explained when he didn't say anything. "I don't expect you to stay...for me."

"Well, that's the thing about expectations. Sometimes they're not high enough."

She gave in to a slow smile that matched his. "Challenge accepted. Next you'll be suggesting we go skiing."

"Don't underestimate yourself, Elise," he said, giving her shoulder a pat. "Now, how about we take Shambles out of her pen for some air, check on the other animals in your Nativity, and then have lunch together. I'm here for the day. Unless you're busy."

"I'm all yours," she said, biting back a laugh because, honestly, she'd never meant anything as much as those words.

Chapter Eleven

MJ

MJ loved the quiet magic of the Ever After Bridal Salon in Park City, where she joined her sister, daughter, niece, and a few friends for Nicole's final wedding dress fitting. The gently lit rooms smelled faintly of pressed satin and perfume, where hopes and dreams lived on satin hangers. She tried her best to embrace the glow, even though her body felt about ten minutes behind her brain and her heart felt...well, a little off-beat.

The salon was a fairy tale of blush pink with gold accents, plush carpets and low-slung velvet sofas set around a small raised platform. Snow drifted lazily outside the tall windows, making everything feel hushed and intimate.

Taking a deep breath, MJ tried to center herself and focus on the moment of her niece's final fitting. The room was filled with the people she loved most—Cindy, of course, excited in her role as mother of the bride after having been the bride just a few weeks earlier.

Nicole was still in the dressing room with the stylist, building anticipation for a group that included Elise and

Brianna, Nicole's closest friend. Next to MJ, Gracie sipped a mimosa and seemed quieter than usual.

"You okay?" MJ whispered, leaning closer to her daughter.

"Oh, yes. You're the one who seems a little...I don't know. Different. Distant."

"Do I?" Dang. She thought she'd been doing such a good job of hiding it. "I'm just not sleeping well."

Gracie eyed her. "Too many late nights with Matt?"

MJ smiled. "Not that late, really. After dinner, we sometimes take a night walk, but...he's not keeping me up."

But *something* woke her at three in the morning.

Before she could consider whether or not to elaborate, the curtain to the dressing suite swished, and the bridal stylist poked her head out.

"She's ready, ladies."

Cindy inhaled sharply. "Am I going to cry again?"

"Yes," they all answered in perfect unison, punctuating the single word with an outburst of laughter.

MJ shook off her thoughts and forced herself to concentrate on the memory they were making. Rising, she went behind the sofa and put her hands on Cindy's shoulders.

"You earned the momma tears, Cin. Enjoy every minute of it."

Cindy dropped her head back and looked up at MJ with an upside-down grin. "I will. I promise."

After a minute of chatter and laughter, Nicole

stepped out slowly, a vision in white as she floated to the platform to a chorus of gasps, oohs, and ahhs.

They'd all loved this gown when she picked it, but now, without the clips and all the buttons up, the effect was truly breathtaking.

The A-line dress fit her like a dream, from the strapless, straight bodice down to the scalloped hem that kissed the floor. It flowed like poured cream, without a snippet of lace or a single pearl, which added to the mix of drama and elegance of a timeless, stunning wedding gown.

"Oh, sweetheart," Cindy breathed, slowly rising to get closer. "You...are...beautiful."

Nicole blinked back her own tears. "Thanks, Mom. It's perfect."

They hugged and the stylist came closer, holding a cathedral veil trimmed with the tiniest gems, inviting Cindy to place it on Nicole's head for the full effect.

As she did, every woman in the room sniffled, wiped tears, and held hands, drinking in the sweet moment.

Stepping back to look at her daughter, Cindy pressed one hand to her heart, her whole face shining with a mother's full, unfiltered joy.

They cooed and fussed some more, taking pictures, giving toasts, laughing as they learned how to bustle the train. It was all so lovely that it took MJ's mind off her problems, making her laugh and enjoy the event.

The stylist helped Nicole down, and the women all gathered around her, admiring the dress from every angle, all voting on a perfect white faux fur wrap to cover her during the obligatory sleigh ride.

When it was over and everyone had gathered their own formal dresses, the group lingered near the front counter, chattering about the wedding weekend, travel times, and whether Copper should wear something "festive" during sleigh photos.

Nicole hugged every single person twice and couldn't stop smiling.

As they said goodbye, Gracie slipped an arm around MJ and pulled her closer. "You'd tell me if something was wrong, wouldn't you?"

MJ laughed softly, knowing that she had never been very good at hiding her feelings, especially from her dear daughter. "I'm fine," she insisted.

"It's not Red, is it? Are you feeling okay? Is it the fact that Nicole is getting married and I'm not?"

MJ gasped at the question. "Gracie! No." But she'd have to give a real answer or her daughter would keep pressing. "Look, it's nothing that needs to pull focus from today."

"So there *is* something." Gracie's brows pinched. "Mom..."

MJ swallowed. "I'll tell you later."

Gracie launched a brow. "Later is...now. Come to Sugarfall with me."

"I have to get back to the lodge," MJ said. "We have so much to do to get ready for the real opening, the wedding, and—"

"Then I'll drive you." Gracie gripped her arm.

"Mom, I know when something's going on with you. Please."

MJ looked through the windows at the slow-falling snow, thinking. Yes. She needed to tell someone, and who better than the daughter she trusted completely?

"Of course," MJ whispered, relief flooding her. "Thank you, honey."

🌲

GRACIE NEARLY DROVE off the road when MJ dropped the bomb that her new third-floor apartment was haunted...by George McBride.

"What?" She steadied the bakery van and merged into traffic with a quick glance at MJ. "You're not serious."

"I'm not...*not* serious. You remember the music box your father gave me when you were born?"

"The white enamel one that plays *What a Wonderful World*? Of course. It's in my bedroom."

"Excuse me?" MJ slammed her palm against her breastbone, shocked. "You *have* it? I've been looking everywhere. I thought I had it."

"Well, it's on my nightstand next to a picture of Dad." She frowned. "You left it when you moved into the lodge after Dad died."

"I don't remember that," MJ admitted. "But then I don't remember much from those days."

"I figured the music box made you sad," Gracie said. "So I kept it for you."

"You have it." MJ squeezed her eyes at what this meant. "So he's not using it to communicate with me."

Gracie's eyes grew wide. "Oookay..." She dragged out the word. "You better be more specific. He's *communicating?*"

"I don't know."

"Mom! Are you serious?"

She let out a sigh, knowing how it sounded, but now there really was no explanation. "Every night at three in the morning—exactly, mind you, not one minute before or after—I hear the song. Digital, like the music box. I thought maybe I'd stuffed it in a drawer or something, but now...you have it."

"Plus, it's not digital," Gracie said. "It's a wind-up music box that wouldn't play by itself."

"Especially if it's on your nightstand," MJ added.

"You must be dreaming, Mom."

"I don't think so," MJ said. "I hear it, loud and clear. Well, not loud and not clear. Almost as if it's underwater."

"Have you looked under sofa cushions and taken everything apart? Checked all the cabinets?"

"Yes, yes. But I was looking for the music box because nothing else would make that noise or play that song." She sighed. "Your father knows what that song means to me."

Gracie considered that, turning off the main highway

toward the lodge. "What do you think he's trying to say, Mom?"

"Well, not that you believe me—"

"I believe you," she said quickly. "But I do think it could be your imagination or even your conscience, thinking Dad would be upset if you fell in love with another man."

"He would be," MJ said.

"I don't think so," Gracie replied.

MJ bit her lip and looked out the window.

"I really don't," Gracie reiterated. "Dad only ever wanted you to be happy. And it's been six years. You're in your early sixties, vibrant and full of energy and optimism. You should have a wonderful partner in your life."

Each word pressed on her heart. "I had a wonderful partner," she said. "But he was taken too soon."

Gracie's eyes shuttered. "That he was."

"And we never expected him to die, so we never talked about...what-ifs."

"Well, what if the situation were reversed?" Gracie asked. "What if you'd left us far too soon? Would you want him to be alone?"

MJ shook her head, having already given this question a lot of thought. "He had a lot of love to give and if the right woman came along—assuming she didn't outcook or outbake me—then, sure, of course I'd want him to spend his golden years with...someone."

The words caught in her throat.

"It's not easy to think about," Gracie agreed, reaching over to add a gentle touch. "But your answer is the same as his would have been. He wants you to be happy and Matt's a great guy."

MJ sighed again, this time with a soft groan. "I know."

"Then why the pain in your voice, Mom?"

"Because Matt's so great, he's…" She shifted in her seat, an emotion eating at her with the same voraciousness that attacked her at three in the morning. "I feel guilty," she whispered, finally getting to what really bothered her. "I feel so incredibly guilty."

"For possibly loving someone else?" Gracie asked. "Why?"

"Because I could love him…a lot. Not that I do yet—well, maybe I do. But I could love Matt in a way that…" She swallowed. "He could be…"

She tamped down the rest because did Gracie need to hear that the new man in her mother's life might actually be…*better*…than the first one? The one who'd given Gracie life? It was unthinkable.

And yet, MJ thought it…a lot.

"He could be what?" Gracie pressed.

"Very special," MJ managed to say.

Gracie was quiet as they neared the lodge, staring at the red light at the intersection, pensive.

"See?" MJ finally scoffed when Gracie didn't say a word even after the light changed and she turned left.

"See what?"

"It's a problem for you, too."

"It's not a problem, Mom. I think it's amazing that you've met someone so spectacular."

"But what do I do when I get to heaven?" MJ almost

wailed, the heart of her question rising up. "Which one will be my husband?"

Gracie slipped her lip under her front tooth, visibly trying not to laugh.

"I'm serious, Gracie!"

"I know you are, but people do get married for a second time and you deserve love and I don't think you'll be punished in the afterlife if you love them both."

MJ dropped her head back and closed her eyes. "And none of this is explaining what he's trying to tell me every single night at three a.m."

Gracie pulled into the lodge's drive and took the van past the ski shed and up the narrow road that wound around all the cabins and past the woods.

"Where are you going?" MJ asked.

"Home to get that music box for you. I mean, maybe I only think it's on my nightstand. Maybe Benny moved it to your apartment for some reason we don't know. Maybe he hid it."

"Why would he do that?"

She threw a look. "It's Benny. He probably made a bet with Red. They get crazy, those two."

Clinging to that hope, MJ nodded. "I hope you're right," she said. "Because if that music box is here, then something otherworldly is playing the song every single night. Some*one*, not some*thing*."

Gracie parked, turned off the van and reached for her seatbelt, looking hard at MJ.

"It's probably your imagination, Mom. A guilty conscience that you shouldn't have. If Matt is spectacular, if he makes you happy and whole and fills your life and your heart forever and ever, I guarantee you Dad wouldn't mind that at all."

MJ wasn't so sure, but she just nodded and followed Gracie into the house. Red and Benny were both out, so they walked through the quiet rooms, up to the second floor.

Long ago, Gracie had moved into the main bedroom, the very room where Irene and Owen Starling had lived, then MJ and George. Now it was Gracie's, charmingly redecorated with shiplap and flowered wallpaper, looking nothing like it had when MJ had slept there every night next to George.

Still, the room hit her hard. The light streaming through the sheers was...familiar. Yes, the colors were brighter and younger, and the furniture was arranged differently, but this was the room where MJ had lived with and loved her husband. Where she'd nursed a baby and heartaches, laughed into the wee hours with her partner, and cried into her pillow when he died.

And there, on top of the nightstand on the side where Gracie didn't sleep, was a picture of George and...the music box.

"Goodness." MJ walked around the bed and slowly dropped down, realizing that she was shaking a little as she reached for the box. "It *is* here."

She lifted it, turning it over to read the inscription.

For MJ ~ You make my world wonderful. Love, George

She closed her eyes and remembered how pleased

he'd been when he gave it to her, so thrilled to have found a music box that played their song at that cute little snow globe store in town.

She twisted the tiny key at the bottom, then grazed the blue flowers on a white enamel top with one fingertip. A little scared for reasons she didn't quite understand, she slowly lifted the lid and heard the familiar strain that Louis Armstrong made famous.

"This isn't what's waking me every night," she whispered, closing it again.

Gracie sat next to her on the bed, a gentle hand on MJ's back. "Obviously, since it's been here for six years."

"The notes are the same, but the one I'm hearing is, like, a computer sound. I didn't realize it until now, when I heard this."

Gracie leaned back on her hands, thinking. "Could you have an alarm set on your phone or something in the kitchen? One of the appliances? Do you ever take your laptop up there?"

She shook her head. "No, and the sound is kind of muffled. It's got to be...George."

Gracie sighed. "How does that make you feel, Mom?"

"Guilty. Scared. Foolish." She ground out the words. "Like your father is watching me and it's very important that he wake me up and tell me that *we* had love, and this is...wrong."

"Mom, Matt is a good man who clearly has strong feelings for you. He won millions and millions of dollars and gave it away to charities and causes—and Snowberry Lodge!"

MJ closed her eyes. He was a good man, but...

"Did you feel guilty before this started?"

"I was too busy wondering whether or not he'd come back," she admitted.

"And when did this start?" Gracie asked. "The music, not the feelings."

"The night Matt got here. The night of Cindy's wedding. I've been sleeping in that apartment for months and never heard it. Then, it started and will not stop."

"It started that night? The night he arrived?" The tone in Gracie's voice was unmistakable.

"You think there's a connection?" MJ asked.

"Well, it's...a coincidence. But..." She made a face. "I just don't believe Dad's coming back to haunt you with music that would make you sad. Not only is it impossible, it's not like him. He'd never hurt you."

MJ nodded, then leaned into Gracie. "I'm really embarrassed at how this weird little thing has wrecked me. It's kind of...ruining things with Matt."

"Does he know?"

"No," MJ said. "I don't want him to think I'm off my rocker or...wallowing in guilt, which might make him back away. He'd probably think I'm scared or foolish."

"Oh, Mom, no. I don't see it that way at all. I mean, I get being a little scared of a new relationship—I'm petrified. But foolish? How?"

"I'm old to...have a crush," she said.

"I don't think crushes have an age range," Gracie told her. "What, exactly, are you scared of?"

She bit her lip. "He wants to move here and buy a house. I don't...know what to do about that."

"You've never lived anywhere but Snowberry from the day you were born," Gracie said. "Do you think if you got married and moved in with him, you'd be giving up... everything?"

"Maybe," she admitted. "I don't know."

"Well, as far as the wake-up call, Mom? I think you have an issue—real or in your heart—and if this man is going to be your partner, he's the person you should talk to. How he reacts will tell you a lot."

"I guess." MJ stroked the music box again and set it back down, next to George's picture. She ran her finger over the frame and looked into his eyes, waiting for that kick of guilt, but feeling nothing but a deep, abiding love.

"You want to take the music box?" Gracie asked.

"You keep it, honey." She stood up and sighed. "I'm glad to know it's here. And I'll find the right time and talk to Matt."

For reasons she didn't quite understand, she was dreading that conversation.

Chapter Twelve

Elise

Elise steadied her breath as the soft whir of the anesthesia machine hummed through the blindingly bright operating room. Shambles lay sedated on the padded surgical table, her coat clipped and her head positioned in a foam cradle. The surgery site smelled faintly of antiseptic and warm wool—a strangely comforting contrast.

Dr. Choi had stopped in earlier, and Millie, a surgical teaching nurse who Elise had befriended through one of her classes, had agreed to come in as back up. Wade was leading this operation, with Elise assisting and learning, mentally taking notes for the paper she'd write about this procedure.

Wade stood opposite Elise, with the surgery table at the perfect height for him to work and for her to see easily from her chair. His posture was relaxed but she could tell his focus was razor sharp, his expression calm, controlled, and confident.

"Ready?" he asked, voice low, steady.

She nodded. "Ready."

"I'm here if you need me," Millie added, coming

closer to the table. "Just keep those eye retractors wide and still, Elise."

She nodded and gripped the device with careful precision as Wade began the delicate cutting and removal of the affected tissue around the sheep's lower eyelid. With each pass of the scalpel, Wade carved millimeter by millimeter.

His hands were beautifully steady, taking breaks as Elise used sterile gauze to dab at fluid or flushed saline into the eye.

"How are you this calm?" she murmured as she watched.

"Practice. Plus, Shambles deserves our A-game."

Her heart clenched at the quiet conviction in his voice. He approached Shambles—an old, dispensable sheep—with the same intensity he might give a prize racehorse.

"Oh!" She gasped at the sight of blood suddenly oozing from the tissue.

"I see it." His tone didn't change. Not one octave. Not even a sigh. "That's...a soft bleeder," Wade said, jutting his chin. "Sterile gauze."

She snagged some in gloved fingers and held out the gauze to him.

"You can do it, Elise."

She swallowed and dabbed the eye, surprised at how much blood came from a "tiny" bleeding vessel. Also a little surprised that she, a disabled graduate student with big dreams and no experience, was on the surgical team.

She'd only hoped that one day she could do this, and

here she was—beating the odds that were stacked against her as strong and high as this wheelchair.

"Is she okay?" Elise asked when she needed a second and third piece of gauze.

"Yes," he assured her. "That vessel wasn't obvious, notably 'soft' because it's not arterial, or catastrophic. A little messy is all."

The bleeding continued—slower, but stubborn. It must have been a deep vessel, and way too close to the lid margin.

A flicker of fear shot through her. If they lost visibility here, if he couldn't cauterize precisely enough... Shambles could lose the eye.

Her stomach tightened as he continued the excision and she worked so that her grip on the retractors didn't tremble.

"Easy," Wade said gently, still not looking away from the surgical field. "Stay with me, Elise."

Elise inhaled and willed her hands to still.

Wade angled the light, shifted his fingers a fraction, and with a controlled motion, cauterized the vessel. The stubborn bleed sizzled, then quieted. This time, he dabbed and, finally, the surgical field cleared.

"You fixed it," she breathed. "I didn't think it could be done."

"We fixed it," he corrected, looking over his mask with a smile in his eyes. "Anyway, lost causes are kind of my thing."

Her pulse skipped. *Lost causes.*

She wondered, fleetingly, if he had any idea how that

phrase felt to someone like her—someone who'd spent fifteen years navigating a world where most people saw her wheels first and her worth second.

He moved on, resecting the remaining carcinoma until it was clean. "You see this margin?" he asked. "That's good tissue. She's going to keep this eye."

"You make it sound easy."

"Nothing worth doing is easy. But nothing is impossible, either."

Some things were, but she kept that to herself as Wade finished the excision, stepped back slightly, and nodded with satisfaction. "Okay. Cryotherapy?"

"The cryoprobe's ready," Millie said, gesturing to the unit. "That's all you need to freeze."

Elise handed him the chilled probe and watched as he applied the instrument to the newly cleared margin. Frost blossomed like delicate ice crystals across the tissue, which was amazing and oddly beautiful.

Wade was made for this, she mused. What would it be like to have a man like Wade Reynolds at her side, made for her, too? She had no idea, but that sure wouldn't stop her from fantasizing about it.

When he finished cryotherapy, Shambles was prepped for recovery, the eye neatly bandaged. Wade removed his gloves and stretched his back with a light groan.

Elise exhaled the breath she'd been holding for... maybe the entire procedure.

"She did great," Wade said, giving the sheep's woolly cheek a pat. "Tough little girl."

"*You* did great," she countered.

His eyes met hers—green, warm, and so full of quiet humility it made her chest ache.

"Couldn't have done it without you, Elise."

Her heart fluttered as they moved Shambles to recovery. The ewe stirred faintly, the sedative wearing off. Elise brushed her wool, whispering, "Good job, girlie," as Wade monitored the vitals.

When Shambles settled peacefully, Wade turned to Elise with a smile that lit up everything inside her.

"Come on," he said. "Let's go do our own recovery over coffee. You look like you're about to vibrate out of that chair."

She laughed—really laughed—and followed him out of the surgical suite.

An hour later, they were across from each other in the Canine Café, each holding a paper cup of coffee, the post-surgical adrenaline dump finally over so they could relax.

"I can't believe we did that," Elise said, inching her chair closer to the table...and Wade. "I mean, I can, obviously, because I was there. But still."

"You were more than there." Wade put his elbows on the surface and pinned her with eyes the color of a Heineken bottle and just as intoxicating. "You were rock solid. I've had residents with three more years of training who shake like leaves the first time they assist. Nurse Millie never needed to step in."

"I *was* shaking," she admitted. "Everywhere except my hands."

"I actually think surgery could be your calling," he said simply.

She thanked him again, the compliment settling on her heart.

He studied her for a beat, eyes crinkling at the corners as his gaze shifted to the windows. In the distance, the rugged peaks rose, white and sharp and beautiful. When he looked back at her, his expression was warm and even a little sad.

"Can I ask you something?" he said.

Oh, boy. Here we go. *How serious is this disability? Is there a cure? Will you ever be...normal? Can you have children?* In other words, *How lost of a cause are you, Elise Hale?*

She braced for all the questions she didn't want to answer, and nodded.

"The other day," he said slowly, "you told me you haven't really dated. Ever. And I... I've been thinking about that and trying to make that make sense in my head. Since you're obviously beautiful, fun, and smart, I'm guessing the decision not to date is yours. Will you change that? Are you willing to...get involved?"

Immediately, her mouth went dry. "Do I have to write a paper on this, too?" she joked.

He laughed. "Maybe a pop quiz later." Then he

leaned closer and lowered his voice. "I want to know if I have a chance."

A *chance?* She gave a quick laugh. "Easy answer, Wade—yes."

"Oh, good." He seemed visibly relieved.

She was relieved, too, that he hadn't asked all the questions—but that didn't mean he didn't have those questions. Now would be as good a time as any to answer them.

"So," she said, dipping one toe into the scary waters of her history and prognosis. "You might have sniffed around enough to know the basics of what, uh, happened to me."

He nodded. "I was chatting with Nicole the other day. I stopped in the ski rental place she runs and I might have casually asked a few questions. I hope you don't mind. I wasn't prying."

She waved it off. "Of course, it's fine." Nicole had texted her that he'd asked more than a few and it didn't seem so casual, so this news was no surprise.

"She just told me there was a bad accident," he added. "If there's anything else you want to share..."

"I always start with this," she said. "From a big-picture standpoint, we were all lucky to live. A jackknifed truck that crossed the lanes might have cost me the ability to walk, but no one in my family was killed, and that's the most important thing to remember."

He searched her face, a million questions in his eyes. "Can you tell me about the injury?"

He sounded like he had in the OR—a medically trained professional—so she went in that direction.

"My legs were crushed in what was considered a lower thoracic incomplete injury at first."

He nodded slowly, not doubt understanding the words and what they meant for a little girl.

"So...that's down around T_{10}, T_{11}, T_{12}. Injuries at that level usually mean you lose motor and feeling from about mid-thigh down." His voice stayed clinical, and careful. "But lower thoracic injuries don't mess with the autonomic system the way higher ones do. That means no blood pressure issues, no temperature regulation problems."

And no bladder and bowel issues, but he was too classy to say that out loud. He was right, though, and it was good news to have those "auto functions" working perfectly. As she often told people—it could have been much worse.

"And as the swelling went down," she continued, grateful for the protection of medical language, "it became clear the injury was functionally complete."

His expression changed again, no doubt because that, in clinical terms, meant she would never walk again. She saw the sympathy in his eyes. Normally hated it, but not with him.

"That had to have been really hard for, what?" He winced. "A ten-year-old girl?"

"Yeah." This single syllable could never convey how hard it had been. Fifteen years ago, she'd dealt with the agony of realizing she'd run, skied, danced, and stood in the shower for the last time. She'd been a child. A terrified, heartbroken, paralyzed kid around the same age as Benny and Olivia.

They'd been the darkest days of her life.

"Honestly," she said quietly, "the emotional pain was way more traumatic than the physical pain."

"How did you cope?" he asked.

"Therapy—physical, emotional, mental. My parents were amazing. My brother was an absolute angel. And I guess I was blessed with a decent attitude in life."

"Not a victim," he said. "I love that about you."

She managed not to react, taking an unsteady breath instead. "By the time I was a teenager, I'd figured out how to do life with a lightweight chair and strong upper-body muscles. I do everything from here up." She tapped the top of her thighs lightly. "And a whole lot from here." She touched her forehead.

He listened like it was the most important case summary he'd ever heard. "I'm...blown away."

"By the injury?" she asked.

"By you. By your determination and spunk and refusal to let a tragedy ruin your life."

She felt some tears sting. No compliment could mean more—he got her. He understood what she'd fought for and felt, right now, at least, like she'd won.

"I just want to live an ordinary life and be a working vet," she said softly. "That was always the dream."

"You are, although nothing about you is ordinary," he said. "Honestly? I forgot you were in a wheelchair in that

OR. All you were was closer to the surgical site and incredibly competent."

"Thank you," she said. "It was fun to watch you work."

He searched her face, thinking. "Have you ever considered...not being in the chair?"

"When I'm in bed," she cracked, "and don't want to get up."

"Seriously, Elise. I'm sure you know there are incredible things happening right now in mobility science. In neurostimulation, AI-assisted exosuits, spinal cord interface breakthroughs. Not guarantees. Just... possibilities."

Her heart squeezed at the gentle hope in his voice, and that familiar, fleeting worry slipped in again—*the fixer of lost causes.*

"For now, I'm happy in school, just being Hale on Wheels, as they call me."

He chuckled. "Cute."

"Cute but...I don't want wheels to be the first thing people see about me. That's why..."

"Why what?" he pressed when she stopped, realizing she'd gone too far. "Elise?"

"Why I was so confident when I met you," she confessed on a whisper. "There was no chair. Just Copper and me, high and mighty in a saddle like a..."

"Like a spirited, stunning, sassy cowgirl," he finished for her.

"Not what I was going to say."

"But it's what I saw."

"Until you saw..." She bit her lip. "The harness."

He shrugged. "Didn't stop me, Elise. I'm a doctor. I see past injuries or medical conditions to the person under it all. And this person?" He reached across the table, taking her hand and stealing her breath. "Is really attractive to me."

This person or...this patient?

She pushed the thought away and let the compliment roll over her like a tidal wave, completely surrendering to the power of it. Had anyone ever said anything like that to her?

No.

"That's...nice." She laughed at the ridiculous understatement. "And it's..." She took a breath, terrified to finish, but wanting so much to say it. "It's mutual."

A slow smile pulled, revealing the shadow of one dimple, perfect teeth, and a light in his eyes that she wanted to get lost in.

"Well, what do you know," he muttered. "Cowgirl likes me. Now what?"

"Now I tell you a little more."

"Please," he whispered. "Tell me everything."

"Okay." She shifted a little, gathering her thoughts, diving into the deep end because she liked him—and trusted him—so much. "I am perfectly capable of living a full, independent life, although it took some work to persuade my family that was true. But I have. And I'm also perfectly capable of... having a normal relationship." Heat crept up her neck, but she pushed through. "Most of my spinal cord is just fine. The parts that make a person...a person? Those work."

He studied her, understanding in his eyes. "Of course they do."

"Try explaining *that* on a first date." She let out a shaky laugh. "Or, you know, even getting to the first date when the guy sees your wheels and panics. It just...felt easier not to try. School was safer. Work was safer. Animals never look at me like that."

"Like what?" he asked.

"Like they're calculating all the things I can't do instead of the things I can." She toyed with the cardboard sleeve on her coffee "So, yeah. Long answer to your question, but that's why I haven't dated."

He nodded slowly, like he was filing every word away. "For what it's worth," he said, "I think any man who can't see past that chair is missing out on a lot. Any guy would be lucky to be the one beside you."

Her heart thudded at that tiny preposition. *Beside you.* Not pushing, not leading. *Beside.*

"You're very...open-minded," she murmured.

"I'm very interested," he corrected. "Is that okay?"

She let herself really look at him then—the tousled hair still damp from the scrub sink, the strong hands that had just saved a sheep's eye, the kindness that never seemed to leave his expression.

"It's...more than okay," she said. "Because I am very interested, too."

"Good. Can I take you out to dinner?"

She laughed, then, buoyed both by the question and the lightning speed that he asked. "Yes," she said. "And maybe I'll even get my first kiss." She winced and covered her face. "Can't believe I just said that."

Slowly, he pushed his chair back and stood. She looked up, uncertainty crawling over her at his serious expression.

Wordlessly, he stepped around the table, came right up to the side of her chair, and lowered himself so they were the same height.

"How about we get that first one out of the way," he said softly. "Because if I don't kiss you right now, I'll spend the next day or so kicking myself."

She took a slow breath, letting her gaze drop to his beautiful mouth, already imagining the feel of his lips.

"May I?" he asked.

She could only nod.

He lifted a hand, giving her every chance to pull back, and then his fingers brushed her cheek, warm and careful and so, so gentle, the hint of antiseptic soap still clinging to him.

He leaned in, eliminating the last inch of space, and pressed his mouth to hers.

The kiss was soft and steady and sure, his lips were warm, tasting faintly of coffee and something uniquely him. He kissed her like she was precious and strong and exactly who she wanted her to be.

For that moment, everything—wheelchairs and scars and old fears—fell away. There was just the feel of him, the quiet of the café, and the dizzy, impossible realization that they genuinely liked each other.

When he finally drew back, it was only far enough to rest his forehead against hers.

"Well," she sighed. "Good to know the whole kissing thing is not overrated."

"And gets even better with practice."

She let out a breathless laugh. "Can't wait."

On a sigh, he pushed to his feet with easy grace. "Let's go check on our patient in recovery, then I'll take you home and we'll plan our practice session—er, dinner date."

Later, after he'd left—and after about five kisses, ten hugs, and a solid plan to go out in a few days—Elise rolled to her mirror and tried to see herself the way Wade Reynolds did.

Spirited, stunning, sassy.

As she replayed his compliments, her whole face seemed to change. She didn't look at herself like a disabled twenty-five-year-old wheeling herself through a sad and sometimes deeply disappointing life.

She was...his cowgirl. Not a project, not a problem, not a lost cause. And that made the whole world look blindingly bright and full of possibilities.

Chapter Thirteen

Red

Red Starling surveyed the chaos exploding across Snowberry Lodge's front parking loop on Christmas Eve afternoon with one simple goal in mind—to get in a vehicle that would not include an hour-long ride next to Bertie Kessler.

With the two kids running around, their dogs barking, and all the women fussing about who'd ride with whom, he knew he had to stake a claim and fast.

Red shoved his gloved hands deeper into the pockets of his coat and planned his move.

Cindy and Jack would bring Bertie, who looked ready to pounce on Red and grill him on the Four Pillars of Longevity again. He'd gotten trapped yesterday and forced into a "gentle incline walk" up the east trail. Gentle? A trip to the bathroom was gentle, God willing. That walk was actual punishment that he still felt in his hips.

Cameron and Nicole? Possibly, but they were probably taking MJ and Matt and then he'd feel like a fifth wheel.

So that left Gracie, who didn't appear to have a ride to the Live Nativity at Great Basin Veterinary Institute.

She was busy with the dogs, checking her phone, keeping an eye on Benny and Olivia, who were currently knee-deep in a snowbank.

He edged sideways—quiet, stealthy, moving toward his granddaughter as she bent over to clip Newt's harness.

Kids and dogs. Yup. These were going to be his people.

He cleared his throat. "You need a passenger, Gracie?"

She looked up and gave him one of her soft smiles. "Of course you come with us, Red," she said, brushing snow off her gloves as she stood. She leaned closer and whispered, "That way you can escape Bertie."

"Am I that obvious?"

"Only because she might make you *walk* to Eagle Mountain just for the cardio."

He snorted. "No might about it."

Gracie grinned. "Marshall is two minutes away and we can all fit in his truck."

"And, uh, his...Olivia's mother?" Bianca was nowhere to be seen, but Red had noticed she could pop up at unlikely times. When he saw her, it made his heart heavy to think he might be holding onto a secret that Gracie or Marshall should know. But he still wasn't sure and he didn't want to speculate.

"She said she doesn't really 'dig' the smell of sheep and goats, and agreed to let Olivia go with us." She grinned. "I promise, you're safe."

Marshall's big black truck pulled up, rumbling up the

hill with a muscular engine. Just the sight of him made Gracie stand taller, warmth blooming in her eyes.

When Marshall hopped out, his gaze scanned the group for Olivia, found her, then instantly shifted to Gracie. Red watched the two of them share a smile that reached both their eyes, the connection as real as a bolt of electricity.

Guilt squeezed his chest. He should warn her that Bianca was really up to no good. He didn't want to see his sweet and trusting granddaughter get smashed under that woman's expensive boot. When could he tell her? *What* could he tell her?

Olivia scampered toward Marshall, arms out, braids flying, "Daddy!" on her lips.

"There's my girl!" He scooped her up and gave her a twirl, but his gaze went right back to Gracie, which only made Red's old heart twist.

Tonight. He was definitely going to find some way to tell Gracie what he might have overheard. She could do what she wanted with that information—maybe nothing —but Red would have a clear conscience.

When Marshall stepped back from Olivia, he turned to Gracie, his whole expression warming even more as he reached for her.

"Merry Christmas Eve, gorgeous," he murmured, both of them standing close enough for Red to hear the exchange.

"Red's going to ride with us, too," Gracie said after she hugged him.

"Awesome! There's plenty of room," Marshall agreed, walking to the back of his truck. "We can put the dogs—"

"Wait! Wait! Don't leave without me!" The high-pitched cry broke over the commotion of car doors and barking, making all of them turn toward the road that led to the cabins.

Bianca Hampton—in a cheetah-print jacket and carrying a handbag that he suspected cost more than his first new car—came teetering across the snow in high-heeled boots.

He felt, rather than heard, a groan of defeat from Marshall.

"I decided I want to go!" she called, waving one hand overhead.

Gracie's face blanched. Marshall's smile vanished. Even Olivia's eyes flashed with a silent *uh-oh*.

Bianca headed straight for Marshall, who subtly leaned back the way people do when a bee lands on their shirt and they're trying not to freak out.

"Oh, my gosh, thank goodness I caught you," Bianca gushed, slipping her hand around his arm like she was boarding one of the *Titanic*'s lifeboats. "Olivia needs *both* her parents tonight. It's Christmas Eve. It's our holiday. Our shared special time. This Nativity...*thing* is such an important family moment."

Red bit back a groan of doom.

Marshall gently extracted his arm. "Bianca...it's *live*, remember? That means...animals that smell and..."

"Poop!" Olivia said, making everyone laugh nervously.

"Right," Marshall agreed. "And you don't look dressed for—"

"I'm fine!" Bianca declared, wobbling prettily. "And, Marsh, it means something to Olivia for me to be there. Family memories? Hello? You want me to go, right, Livvie my love?"

The little girl let out a puff of breath, looking helplessly from one parent to the other. "Yeah...sure. I just don't think it's actually your...um, scene, Mom."

"Then I'll make it my scene," she declared.

Or she would make *a* scene, Red thought.

Marshall cleared his throat. "I'm taking the kids and the dogs and Gracie. And Red, so I don't really have room."

If Red hadn't heard what he thought he heard while he'd been hiding in that cabin, he'd have shown some class and instantly volunteered to ride with Jack and Cindy. But that would play right into this viper's schemes.

Bianca clapped two hands dramatically over her heart. "But Marshall, it's Christmas Eve! And I am *legally* supposed to be with her, so I'll just keep her here with me and we'll sit in the cabin alone."

"Bianca." He ground out her name in a way that sounded...like he'd said it that way a million times. "You can't—"

"Just take me, Marsh. I can't let her go without me. I *need* to be with her."

Red rolled his eyes so hard he nearly saw his brain stem.

Marshall held firm. "Bianca, this event is very...small-town."

"Right? Like I'm in my own Hallmark movie. Let's get great pictures for my social media accounts." She pushed by him, undaunted and clueless. "Olivia! Let's go, honey."

Marshall was visibly torn—a good man and a good father. It was obvious he wanted Gracie next to him. But Bianca was digging in with talons.

Gracie stepped forward, her face the picture of the very word she was named for...grace.

"It's okay, Marshall," she said. "Take Bianca and the kids. They'd hate to be separated tonight. I'll drive with Red in the Sugarfall van."

Marshall looked pained. "Gracie, no. Absolutely not."

Bianca perked up, smug as a cat under a heat lamp. "Now, there's a plan."

"No, truly," Gracie insisted, hiding her hurt like a pro. "You take the kids." Her voice lowered. "It's her Christmas Eve, Marshall. It's fine."

Red could see it wasn't fine at all.

Marshall tried again. "Gracie—"

"I'll follow behind," she said, already turning. "See you there!"

Bianca practically floated into the truck, tossing her hair and trilling on about getting the right picture.

Gracie pasted on a smile that fooled absolutely no one as she and Red walked to the van.

The good news, Red decided as he pulled on a seatbelt—besides not being stuck with Bertie—was a chance to talk to Gracie alone and honestly.

They pulled away from the lodge, a light snow swirling in the van's headlights.

For a full minute, Gracie said nothing, just stared straight ahead, her jaw set.

Red finally broke the silence. "You okay, kiddo?"

"No," she said bluntly. "I mean...yes. I mean...ugh. Grandpa, I'm crazy about that man and he, well..."

"It goes both ways," Red said simply. "A blind man could see how he feels about you."

She sighed and gave a wistful smile. "I think you're right. And he did want to spend this holiday together to see how serious this relationship could be. But that was when he thought Olivia would be in California with Bianca and we'd have some real quality time." Her voice cracked. "Then Bianca blows in like a blizzard and we are...hijacked."

Red made a sympathetic grunt. "She's truly a pest who won't go away."

Gracie moaned. "I'm trying so hard to respect that she's Olivia's mother—I *really* am. But she *bulldozes* over everyone and everything."

Red stared out the windshield, debating what and how to tell his tale. His stomach twisted.

Gracie glanced over. "You're quiet. That's never good."

He grunted. "I'm thinking."

"About what?" she pressed. "Red? Are you all right? Do you feel sick or..."

He rubbed his hands on his thighs. "I'm fine. But, I gotta tell you something, and you're gonna think…" He huffed out a breath. "I don't know what you're going to think, but if I don't tell you, I'll go crazy."

"Red." Her voice dripped with sympathy and worry. "You can tell me anything. You know that."

He shifted and pulled the blasted seatbelt off his chest, wishing for the days when those things were optional. "I overheard something weird the other day."

She frowned, waiting.

He sighed dramatically. "Because I was, uh, hiding in Bianca's cabin."

Gracie nearly swerved. "*Excuse me?*"

He threw both hands up. "Not on purpose! I ducked in because I was escaping Basic Training with Bertie. I literally hid from her in the first available place—moments before you and Bianca entered the cabin. I was in the hall bathroom."

Gracie slapped a hand over her mouth, laughing. "Oh, my gosh, no! Red Starling, you are something else!"

"What I am is troubled by what I heard after you left."

Some color left her cheeks as she peered at the road ahead. "What did you hear?"

"It was muffled by the door and her movement, but I heard her talking on the phone to someone by the name of Tara—I think. That's the thing about all of this—it's based on speculation and eighty-three-year-old ears, so take it all with a boulder of salt."

"Tara is her sister, so you got that much right." Gracie slid him a questioning look. "What did she say?"

"So, there was a lot of giggling and stuff, but some of the bits and pieces I heard…"

"Yes?"

"About her high credit cards."

Gracie nodded. "I get the impression she's up to her eyeballs in debt. Not sure why you think that's troubling for anyone but her."

"Because of the way she might be trying to, uh, get out of it."

Tapping the brakes, Gracie swallowed. "How?"

"Like I said, I could be wrong. My ears are old, her voice is shrill, and she was fussing on the other side of a bathroom door."

"Red," she said impatiently. "Tell me."

"Sounded like she either might have a little bun in the oven or is planning to get one, and hoping that her former husband will, um, either be the baby daddy or think he is. I don't know because—"

"*What?*" Gracie choked.

"I could just be imagining all that," he said quickly, because the words sounded so preposterous. "I mean, she's obviously got an agenda and I'm just saying the word 'baby' was bandied about a good bit, and she said things like 'baby needs a daddy and he's my best option.' What would you make of that?"

"I don't…even know what to say," Gracie stuttered. "Are you sure? What exactly do you remember? Please, Red, I need specifics."

He moaned and snapped the seatbelt, digging through his memory of the moment to recall specifics. "She said this was her 'best shot' and that she might go to jail."

Gracie gasped.

"But the woman is given to the dramatic," Red added.

"Ya think?" she replied dryly. "Anything else?"

"She said she spent every dime of alimony and that was...why she is here."

"Good heavens." Gracie's eyes shuttered. "Why didn't you tell me this?"

He winced with guilt. "Because I'm not sure I heard all that...exactly. And it seems extreme and not my place and Marshall's smart and he can see through her and..." He grunted. "I'm sorry, Gracie. I just knew I was out of line."

"*She's* out of line!" she retorted. "Way, way. Now what do I do?"

"I guess you tell Marshall and he can confront her."

"Oh, goodness, he already has trust issues."

"With her, not you," Red fired back. "And you don't have to tell him anything specific about babies and such. Just let him know that she has an agenda."

"He knows that," she said. "He knew it when she showed up on day one. This won't surprise him. Maybe it will, but I don't know. Also, you heard it eavesdropping through a bathroom door."

He gave her a look. "Right? So now you understand why I've kept this to myself. I might have heard it wrong. I don't trust my ears. Wax buildup. Age. Echo in the bathroom. Could've been talking about a TV show or another friend. I missed some things."

Gracie sighed. "Or...she's pregnant and plans to seduce him and make him think the baby is his."

"Or that," he agreed.

They sat in silence as the van rumbled down the highway.

"I don't know what to do," she finally said, clearly struggling in the very way Red had wanted to avoid.

"Benny wanted to stick Bigfoot on her," he muttered.

"You told this to Benny?" she asked, aghast.

"No, no, no. But Benny's smart and he talks to Olivia, and they think she wants to get back in Marshall's good graces, maybe get him to leave and move to California and be a family again. Or Bianca would move here. Benny thinks she's going to ruin everything."

"She could. Benny is right. What's this about...did you say Bigfoot?" She gave a quick laugh. "And why am I not surprised?"

"He said she's afraid of wildlife, so he was thinking he'd scare her out of town. Raccoons, bears, or..."

"Bigfoot," Gracie finished. "It would probably get rid of her." She started laughing and threw him a look. "It's so something you and that kid would do together."

"I'll have you know that I put the old kibosh on Bigfoot," Red said proudly. "Bein' the responsible adult and strong male authority in his life, I figured it was best."

She smiled. "That you are, and I'm grateful for it."

Red blew out a breath. "I'm getting old for that job, Gracie. My days...are numbered."

"Stop it," she said, all humor gone from her voice. "Don't even say that, Red."

"You know it's gonna happen sooner or later."

"Later," she whispered. "Much, much later. You're going to see Benny graduate from high school, college, and win the Nobel prize in physics."

He wanted to chuckle at that, but the moment felt too serious.

"Look, honey." He leaned over the console to make his point. "I'm fine with whatever the good Lord decides for me. The fact is, I am the man in that kid's life and in all my years, I've never loved a role more."

"You're sweet, Red."

"I'm a lot of things, Gracie, but sweet ain't one of 'em. Anyway, I want a good man in your life—for you *and* Benny. I think Marshall is a fine candidate for the job. So this woman is really upsetting the apple cart and she's dangerous and I don't like her."

"Neither do I," Gracie said, turning off the highway to Eagle Mountain, the lights of the valley twinkling below as the van wound down the snowy mountain road.

The world outside glowed with Christmas magic—frosted trees, soft snowfall, car headlights weaving through the night.

As they pulled into the GBVI parking area, Red reached over and patted her hand.

"What are you going to do?" he asked. "Tell all this to Marshall?"

She shrugged. "I guess—I'm not sure. I don't know what else to do."

"There's always Bigfoot," Red joked.

She eyed him suspiciously. "You're kidding, right?"

"You can never know with me, can you?"

"Nope. But I love you." She gave him a warm look, then hugged him. "And no man could ever be a better role model for Benny. I mean that."

He held onto the words, feeling the weight of the secret leaving his shoulders, and his heart...well, the old ticker felt good and strong for the first time in a few weeks.

That's what doing the right thing did for a man.

Chapter Fourteen

Gracie

For one perfect moment, it felt like the whole world smelled like hot cocoa and Christmas Eve magic. Also wet sheep, hay, and something at the very back of the manger that Gracie preferred not to inhale.

Scents aside, the Live Nativity was one of the most beautiful things Gracie had ever seen.

They launched with a play that retold the entire story of the birth of Jesus, including Mary arriving on a very confident donkey, with much singing from a choir of angels, and—to the delight of the crowd—a real baby in white swaddling.

While they watched and listened, Gracie sat next to Benny, her hand on his back as the message and moment pressed on all their hearts. When the angels sang *Silent Night*, there wasn't a dry eye in the place, including Olivia, who rested her head on her father's shoulder in a move that melted Gracie's heart.

After the performance, the whole set was open for people to walk through, take pictures, and pet the animals. Lights twinkled overhead and snow floated down in gentle flurries that looked too perfectly timed to be real.

Off to the side, Elise beamed at all of them like a proud mama, tugging a faux fur wrap around her. Wade stayed close to her, and they both happily guided the family to meet Shambles, who was clearly their favorite star of the show.

The old ewe bleated at Benny and nuzzled a delighted Olivia while Elise explained why she had a patch on her eye.

As they moved through the stalls and met the animals, Marshall stayed close to Gracie, making comments and jokes and doing his level best to ignore Bianca—a woman who didn't get ignored very often.

Benny and Olivia stood pressed against the rails, faces glowing from the cold and pure joy, their mittened hands waving at the goats like they were celebrities.

"This is the best one yet!" Benny declared, nearly vibrating as he pointed at Eeyore. "That donkey winked at me. That means good luck. It's, like, scientifically proven."

"It is not scientifically proven," Olivia said, though she was bouncing, too. "But it was really cool."

Gracie smiled, warmth blooming in her chest. Christmas Eve, a Live Nativity pulled off flawlessly, her family all around her...and Marshall standing close enough that his coat brushed her sleeve whenever he shifted. If she turned her head just slightly, she could feel his breath mix with the icy air.

It should have been perfect.

But there was Bianca, lingering a few steps away like an unwelcome shadow. She all but batted her lashes at

Marshall, announcing how much she "loved anything wholesome and cozy," as though she were doing an interview for the local paper.

Marshall moved away in a subtle but unmistakable inch backwards—one Gracie doubted Bianca noticed.

Gracie tried to focus on the animals, the lights, the kids, the music, but Red's story kept replaying in her head.

Maybe Bianca didn't say what he thought. Maybe she was talking about a TV show or... some terrible reality program. Maybe she's late on her period and just complaining to her sister. Maybe she's joking in bad taste. Red could have misunderstood.

Except Red wasn't prone to imagination.

And Bianca was...*Bianca.*

Gracie exhaled a shaky breath that fogged the air in front of her, so frustrated that the night couldn't just be lovely and uncomplicated. Determined to enjoy the moment, she joined Elise, Wade, Nicole, and Cameron as they fussed over Shambles.

"Hi, Gracie," Elise called, the sheep's head nuzzling against her chest. "I think Benny loved this, don't you?"

"He's in heaven." She leaned down and hugged her. "This event was incredible. Seriously. People were glowing watching it. You pulled off a masterpiece, Elise."

Elise's eyes twinkled with genuine joy and a little sparkle eyeshadow. "The whole thing was really special," she agreed. "I already got roped into running it again next year."

Something in the way she said that made Gracie think Elise didn't mind the work at all.

Behind them, Wade was talking to Matt, laughing with his uncle, chatting with Gracie's mom, who looked… troubled. Still? Hadn't she talked to Matt about the music yet?

Gracie stepped closer to MJ. "Hey, Mommy," she said in a teasing voice. "How are you?"

Her mother sighed and lifted a shoulder. "Tired."

"It hasn't stopped?"

"Every morning at three a.m. on the nose."

"Did you tell Matt?" Gracie asked.

She shook her head. "What can he do, honey? Other than think I'm a lunatic."

"He could understand that it's troubling you," she said, and even as she did, she felt the words hit her hard. She had to talk to Marshall, too. He needed to know what was troubling her, just like Matt did.

"I guess," her mother said. "But I've been avoiding it."

"You shouldn't," Gracie said, as much to herself as to MJ. "If you can't have hard conversations, are you really a couple?"

MJ gave a wistful smile, then looked past Gracie, her brows rising. "Look at that," she whispered so softly, Gracie barely heard her.

She followed her mother's gaze, landing on Elise. Wade stood next to her, a possessive and warm hand on her shoulder as he explained to Matt how "they" had performed eye surgery on Shambles.

"Love is in the air," Gracie said under her breath.

"And so's the sheep dung." Bianca walked right up between them, holding out her phone. "Can you get a family shot of the Hamptons, Grace?"

She didn't know what irritated her more, being called Grace—a sin only her ex committed—or being asked to photograph *the Hamptons*.

"One of the goats is eating Grandpa's beard!" Benny shouted from a stall a few feet away.

"I gotta see!" Olivia started running that way, but Bianca snagged her jacket.

"Not yet. We're getting a family photo. Marsh?" She latched onto his sleeve.

Turning, he tugged at Kat's leash. "You get one with Olivia. I've got the dog."

"We'll get one with the dog," she said, drawing all of them together toward the back wall. "Oh, this is rustic. Get a few shots, Grace," she ordered. "Make them Instagram-worthy, please."

Marshall gave her a look that was openly apologetic. "If you don't—"

"It's fine," Gracie assured him.

"A family picture," Bianca added brightly. "Me, Marshall, and Olivia. And Dog."

"Her name's Kat," Olivia said, making a face.

"Wait. Wait." Bianca looked behind her. "Too rustic. In fact, I hate this wall." She glowered at the weathered slats of the barn wall as though they offended her. "No, this won't do. Let's go back by the Nativity scene. With the star. Come on."

Marshall sighed. "Bianca, I don't think—"

"Please." Bianca grabbed Marshall and tugged him away. "It's Christmas Eve. One quick picture. For Olivia's scrapbook."

"I don't even *have* a scrapbook," Olivia muttered.

All the while, Gracie stood there holding the woman's phone, feeling like an employee. But she followed Marshall's lead as he demonstrated class and the ability to smooth over any situation.

They walked back out to the Nativity scene, though Marshall's shoulders were stiff as two boards. Olivia trudged after them, clearly annoyed. Benny ignored the whole thing, still obsessed with the beard-eating goat.

Swallowing the metallic taste of discomfort, Gracie mentally vowed not to be territorial. She wasn't going to be the insecure girlfriend. She wouldn't give Bianca even one ounce of satisfaction.

She lifted the phone. "Okay...smile."

Marshall attempted something that resembled a polite smile. Olivia tried, but there was a hint of her signature eyeroll in the shot. Bianca beamed as though posing for a magazine cover—chin lifted, jacket suddenly open and sliding down one shoulder, a hand on Marshall's arm like she owned him.

Gracie framed the shot just as a text popped up at the top of the screen.

She tried not to read it, she really did. But there it was, from Tara, center of Bianca's phone screen.

Tara: *Did you do it yet?? Time is ticking! You're almost 6 weeks!! Don't chicken out—go for it, girl.*

Gracie's breath froze in her chest.

The phone wobbled in her hands. She nearly dropped it into the snow. Her fingers went numb around the smooth case.

Red hadn't misheard. Bianca really *was* pregnant. And she was here to make Marshall believe the baby was his.

The world tilted. The cold bit into her face. She couldn't move, couldn't blink, couldn't breathe. Questions ricocheted inside her skull. How could she tell him without looking like a jealous snoop?

It didn't matter. He needed to know.

"Gracie?" Marshall's voice cut through the fog. "Everything okay?"

She blinked, forced her jaw to unclench, raised the phone. "Sorry. Just—a snowflake in my eye."

She snapped the picture. The flash lit the scene too brightly. Bianca rushed over and snatched the phone back without thanks, already flipping through the photos.

"All right!" Bianca chirped, apparently satisfied with how she looked in each. "Now one with Marshall and me."

"No, we're done," Marshall announced, putting an arm around Gracie. "You want to step back into the barn? Are you cold?"

"Not in there!" Bianca exclaimed, waving her hand under her nose. "The smell of those animals is making me nauseous."

Well, *something* was making her nauseous. Something...*six weeks along.*

Everything in Gracie's head was muted, muffled, and

her heart hammered so loud she wondered if Marshall could hear it.

Then Olivia tugged his sleeve. "Daddy? Can you please stay at Snowberry tonight? *Pleeeease?* It won't be Christmas morning without you, and I want to go to the big cozy lodge and the tree and everyone there and it'll be perfect and we'll open presents and—"

"Olivia," Marshall said softly. "I don't want to impose—"

"You wouldn't be," Gracie said quickly, hoping that would give them a chance to talk. "Really. We have a few open cabins. You should stay."

Olivia cheered.

"Are you sure?" he asked.

She nodded. "Absolutely."

Bianca perked up like she'd just been offered a golden ticket. "Oh! Well, that works out perfectly. And you don't have to use another cabin, Marsh. We have plenty of room in ours, don't we, Liv?"

"No," Marshall cut in gently but firmly. "I'll stay in an empty cabin...for Olivia."

Bianca's smile faltered. "Oh. Right. Of course. I just... thought maybe for Christmas—"

Marshall didn't budge. "No."

"But you must come over for hot chocolate and the midnight present. You remember the midnight present, right, Olivia?"

"Oh, yeah! Daddy, you have to come and we all open one present at midnight just like old times."

Gracie's stomach churned. He'd be with them until midnight...so, when would they talk?

As they made their way toward the parking lot, fresh snow covering the walkway, Bianca teetered on her ridiculous heeled boots. Navigating the asphalt, she suddenly slid, losing her balance.

Marshall instinctively reached out, catching her by the elbow. Of course, Bianca melted against him with a little breathy laugh.

"Oh, my gosh, thank you," she murmured, head against his shoulder.

Marshall immediately stepped back, his hands raised as though distancing himself from radiation. "Watch the ice."

But the image of Bianca leaning against him, Marshall steadying her, seared into Gracie's brain. They were a family, albeit a broken one. Olivia deserved this, and her midnight present.

They all made their way toward the cluster of cars, laughing, talking, corralling kids and animals and joking about the goat that tried to steal Red's glove.

She'd tell Marshall tomorrow, later in the day, after presents and breakfast. Maybe they'd take a walk and talk. Certain that was the right plan, Gracie turned to where the three of them were, trying not to watch Bianca as she glued herself to Marshall's side.

But it was impossible not to see her whispering to Marshall. Gracie couldn't hear the words, but she saw the shift in Marshall's face—soft, familiar, the look people get when someone references a memory they share.

Bianca laughed quietly. "How about the year when Olivia was three and you had to—"

"Build the tricycle from hell," Marshall finished, chuckling.

"I had to break into the neighbor's garage for a tool. Do you remember, Marsh?"

He nodded, his laugh growing hearty. "Yeah. I remember. Their alarm went off and the Wilsons almost called the police."

"I remember!" Olivia said, dancing.

"No way," Marshall replied. "You were three."

"But I do remember, Daddy." She slid between her parents with a little hop in her step. "I woke up and you both came up to my room and said Santa set off the alarm and he'd be at our house next, so I had to go back to sleep, so you both got in my bed. I think about that every year on Christmas Eve."

Gracie's throat tightened at the music of their laughter.

Bianca wasn't just a random nuisance. She was the mother of Marshall's child. They had a history, a tapestry of life together.

And now, with a pregnancy looming like a storm cloud, the strong threads of that tapestry might pull him back into something Gracie couldn't compete with.

Gracie forced a smile amid the calls of "Merry Christmas" and "be safe," but her insides were churning as a gray, uncertain shadow slipped into her heart.

Chapter Fifteen
Elise

E lise could still feel the warmth of the sweet success on her cheeks, even after the lights around the campus quad had been shut down for quite a while. The glow lingered, humming under her skin like she'd swallowed a star.

The Live Nativity had been a wild, improbable triumph.

Even Eeyore kept his braying to respectable limits and carried Mary with true grace. The hay bales stayed upright. The angels didn't push over the manger. The choir had knocked it out of the park.

And Shambles, the beautiful miracle sheep, trotted out with her new patch around the eye Wade had saved, like a queen wrapped in wool. Her owner had been in tears when he thanked them for saving her sight.

"This was unreal." Nicole threw her arms around Elise, nearly knocking a headband of tinsel off. "Seriously. I'm so proud of you. That was the cutest thing I've ever seen."

"Agreed," Cameron added, and then leaned down to hug Elise carefully from behind her chair. "You pulled off an amazing night, E."

"Thanks, Camelot," Elise whispered, her throat tightening at the pride in her brother's eyes. "And one week from tonight, you two will pull off another amazing event."

Cam and Nicole looked at each other with that glint Elise was used to seeing in their eyes.

"We will?" he joked.

"What are we doing?" Nicole asked.

"It's New Year's Eve. Want to go crazy and get married?" Cam kissed her on the lips. "Pretty please?"

Nicole just laughed and gave him a hug. As they joked around, Elise glanced over at the barn where Wade stood talking to the vet students who'd played Joseph and the innkeeper. He winked when he caught her eye, making her stomach flutter. Butterflies? No, these were full-on Christmas cardinals taking flight.

Her parents were nearby, talking with one of the professors. They kept looking over with soft, melty eyes that clearly communicated how they felt about tonight. Deep, strong pride in their daughter, which made her feel like she'd been dipped in warm chocolate and life was nothing but goodness.

"Hey," Cameron said quietly, pulling her attention back. He leaned down so his face was even with hers. "Can we talk for a second?"

"Sure." Elise turned her chair to face him. "What's going on?"

Nicole squeezed Elise's arm. "I'm going to say goodbye to my mom and dad. I'll be right back." She kissed Cameron quickly and darted away.

Cameron stayed beside Elise, rubbing his gloved hands together for warmth. "So…I've been watching you tonight."

"Creepy," she teased.

"I mean it. I haven't seen you like this in—" He exhaled as he straightened. "—a long time. Maybe ever."

"Like what?"

"Happy is kind of an understatement," he said simply. "Actually, my little sister is radiant."

Her eyes stung instantly at the tone, which was bittersweet and hopeful. "Cam…"

"And I've also been watching *him*." He jutted his chin toward Wade. "Man of the hour."

She snorted. "Is that what he is?"

"You tell me what he is, E. Other than a good guy and a decent vet—I can see all that."

"He's…" Warmth bloomed deep in her chest. "He's certainly got my attention," she finished, getting the expected look of uncertainty from Cam.

"So what does that mean?"

"I don't know," she admitted. "But I like it. And him."

"So do I," Cameron said, the three words lifting her heart. "He seems solid. He watches out for you, makes room for you, includes you without making a big show of it. The good kind of protective. Of course, he lives in Alabama."

"He does," she conceded.

"I mean, there's letting you be independent in Eagle Mountain and there's…impossible."

She blew out a breath. "You, oh great patrolman of

the slopes, are officially in front of your skis. We've... barely kissed."

His eyes flickered at the word *barely*, but he nodded. "I'd say be careful, but that's just dumb. What I will say is this—you deserve everything in the world, Elise. The best guy, the truest love, the greatest life. You never need to compromise on that, or not realize your worth."

There was no way to stop the tear, so she just wiped it away. "I adore you, you know that?"

"Obviously." Cameron smirked, but his smile grew genuine. "I love you, too, E."

Her heart folded as she reached for his hand and squeezed. "Same, Camelot."

Nicole drifted back and they said goodbye with more hugs. Elise promised to be at the lodge with Mom and Dad after she got a little extra sleep on Christmas morning.

After that, Elise went back into the barn where she spotted Wade with Shambles, dragging a bale of hay into her stall, talking softly to his favorite patient.

"Look at her," she said as she wheeled into the stall. "She was perfect tonight and she could see all her adoring fans, thanks to you."

Wade dusted hay off his jacket. "Thanks to us," he corrected. "Are you done here or do you stay until the last four-legged actor is asleep?"

"I'm just about done. The set gets broken down next week sometime. My parents have the van and I'm going back to Heber City with them after I finish closing up this place."

"I'll help you," he said.

Together, they passed every stall while the last of the visitors left. They stopped together and talked to each animal, giving some treats and attention. He talked to each creature with love, remembering their role in the play, checking hooves and hay bales.

That alone made her chest feel full.

When they finished, Wade shoved his hands into his coat pockets. "I had an interesting talk with Luis Mendes."

"Our dean? I barely had a minute with him. What did you talk about?"

"How much I love Great Basin Vet Institute."

Her eyebrows rose. "Really?"

"I do," he said. "And...did you know he's thinking about opening an oncology department next year?"

She sucked in a soft breath. "I didn't know that."

"I told him about my residency at Auburn and he..."

When he didn't finish, she looked up at him. "He... what?"

"He was interested in possibly having me coordinate a residency program here once he hires a department head."

For a moment, it felt like her whole body went numb, not just her legs. "Here?"

He pulled over an overturned feed bucket closer and sat beside her chair, their shoulders nearly touching.

"Would that be so bad, Elise?"

"It would be..." She thought about all the words she could use. Amazing. Wonderful. Miraculous. Dreamy.

Even...impossible. "Nice," she finished, protecting her feelings with the simple word, but hating how lame it sounded.

He gave a dry laugh. "Nice for me...or you...or the school...or..."

"You want me to say it, Wade?"

"Yeah." His voice was rough, but he took her hand and grazed her knuckles with his thumb, and nothing about that touch was rough.

"It would be nice for..." She swallowed and held his gaze. "Us."

"*Yeah.*" This time he dragged the word out and smiled. "That's what I wanted to hear."

She chuckled. "You're, uh, not sure how I feel? Please."

He just looked at her, his bottle-green eyes warm and inviting. "Hey, a guy can hope, but there's never any guarantee with a beautiful blond cowgirl."

She rolled her eyes. "I'm officially in the crush stage," she admitted. "You?"

"I kinda cruised by crush on our first date. Bypassed attraction in the OR. I'm officially into a heavy 'like' and hoping it just gets better."

Was this really happening? She bit her lip to keep from giggling like a schoolgirl. "Things are definitely looking in your favor, Dr. Reynolds."

He leaned in and closed the space between them, punctuating the heady conversation with an even more dizzying kiss.

"So..." He said when they broke apart. "Speaking of

high hopes and the future, I've also been doing a little research."

She blinked at the surprise change of topic. "On sheep or local vet oncology practices or...what?" She couldn't wait to hear his next take on what might be ahead for them.

He let out a long exhale, his breath fogging in the cold. "I've been waiting for the right moment. You have time or are your parents ready to go?"

She glanced at the door. "They ran into some old friends from my horseback riding days and are gabbing with them. Go on."

What else could he say? He'd just admitted he liked her and would consider a job here. What was left? She lifted her chin, bracing for something beautiful.

"I've found out about some amazing studies on spinal injuries. Specifically, functionally complete thoracic injuries. I didn't want to bring it up until I had solid options—real science, not junk stuff."

"Oh." Her stomach gave a small, warning pinch.

"So I talked to an old college buddy of mine," he rushed on, missing the shift in her voice. "I remembered he did a fellowship with a team studying peripheral nerve interfaces in humans. Have you heard of neural cuffs?"

She shook her head, a tight little motion, not trusting her voice.

"What they've done is just incredible," he said, his excitement ramping up as hers did the opposite. "They wrap around damaged nerves and send signals past the lesion. Paired with a brain-computer interface, patients can control movement below their injury. It's early-stage in people, but the data?" He shook his head, awestruck. "It's unbelievable. Some folks regained voluntary knee motion."

Her breath froze in her lungs as the first real words started to form in her head.

He wants to fix me.

"And that's just the first thing," he continued, not noticing her stiffen or the fact that she hadn't said a word or reacted with the slightest...interest. "There's also this stem-cell protocol—guided regeneration near the injury site. They use induced pluripotent stem cells. It could repair micro-damage. Combine that with epidural electrical stimulation and—"

"Wade..." Her voice was barely a breath.

"And the robotics!" he barreled on, enthusiasm blinding him. "AI-driven gait tech. It reads micro-signals from your quads and translates them so you can walk with an exo-frame. Elise, you could hike, or dance, or—"

"Wade."

That time, her voice cracked and he finally stopped.

Confusion knit his brow. "What's wrong?"

Elise blinked hard, fighting the sting in her eyes. "Why...why are you telling me all this?"

"Because I thought you'd want to know." He leaned closer. "This is life-changing stuff. Real possibilities. I just...I wanted you to have hope."

He wanted her to have hope—or he needed it himself?

"Hope for what?" she asked.

"For—" He swallowed. "For walking. Or standing. Or just...having more mobility and independence."

Her entire body went icy. The barn, the falling snow, the warm light—all of it faded under the weight of his words.

"Do you think I'm not independent now?"

"What? No—Elise, no, that's not what I mean."

"You've been researching." Her voice trembled. "Calling people. Studying things. Because you think I need to be fixed."

His eyes widened. "Elise, no. That's not—"

"You literally said these treatments could help me have...hope. Make me normal, I suppose you mean." Her voice cracked again. "So what am I now?"

"I didn't mean it that way."

"But that's how it felt." Her throat closed. "Like you see me as a lost cause you want to save."

Wade shook his head. "I would never—"

"You said that in the OR," she continued. "That lost causes are your thing. That's why you do oncology. And tonight, when you're talking about all this research...it feels like I'm the lost cause *du jour*."

"No! I'm not trying to fix you. I'm trying to help. To give you options. That's what we're both trained to do."

"But you didn't ask if I *wanted* options." Tears burned behind her eyes. "You didn't ask if I'm okay with who I am now."

He froze, some color draining from his cheeks.

"You assumed," she said. "You assumed that I want to

be fixed or saved or…improved. Or maybe it's worse than that."

He winced. "Worse?"

"Maybe you can't think about an 'us' until both of us are…normal."

Wade inhaled like she'd struck him. "Elise, that's not it. I—I love seeing you exactly as you are." His voice shook. "I wasn't saying you needed anything. I was excited and stupid and I should've asked first."

But the damage was already threading its way deep into her heart.

"I can't do this conversation right now." She turned her chair toward the open barn doors.

"Elise—please—"

"My parents are waiting." She grabbed the excuse and prayed it was true as she wheeled outside. Snowflakes kissed her cheeks as she looked around the dark for her parents, who were across the quad near the firepit, deep in conversation with old friends.

She headed that way, everything quiet except for the noisy, horrible, not *normal* crunch of her wheelchair rolling over fresh snow.

"Elise!" Wade hurried after her, reaching her side quickly. "I didn't mean any of it the way it sounded."

She didn't turn. "Then why were you researching? Why look up ways to fix me?"

"Because I care. Because I…I wanted to help."

"By changing me?" She wiped her cheeks with her sleeve. "By making me someone who can fit into your world?"

"That's not fair."

"Maybe not," she conceded, her breath coming out in shaky puffs. "But that's how it feels."

"Elise, I don't want to change anything about you," Wade insisted. "Nothing. I swear. I just got excited about possibilities. I thought I was giving you good news."

"Well, you made me feel like I'm not enough," she said. "And do you really think I don't know about some of those things? That I haven't looked into...all the possibilities?"

"I don't know," he admitted. "We haven't talked about it and that is entirely on me. I should have asked you first. Hundred percent. I'm sorry."

She eyed her parents, watching them rise to say goodnight to their friends. Her eyes shimmered with tears she could no longer blink away.

"This was all too good to be true," she whispered. "I should've known."

"Elise—please—don't say that. I care about you. I want to be with you."

"You want to *fix* me," she said softly, wheeling toward the firepit. "That's not the same thing. Good night, Wade."

"Will I see you tomorrow?"

She looked up at him, seeing the hurt and worry in his eyes, believing he was sorry, but that didn't make this ache any less.

"I don't know," she said. "Thank you for the help. Merry Christmas."

She got a glimpse of his face as she rolled away, the look in his eyes absolutely heartbreaking.

Who was she kidding? What made her think a guy like Wade Reynolds would want...a cripple?

Somehow, like she always did, she managed to bury her pain and the loss of the life she was supposed to have. She smiled and gave a wave to her parents, whose love had never wavered whether she walked or wheeled.

That's what she needed in her life—not someone who wanted to *change* her. She couldn't be changed, and if Wade Reynolds couldn't accept that, then he was not the man for her.

There might never be a man for her, she knew, and that was just...fine.

Chapter Sixteen
MJ

Silent night, holy night.

Snowberry Lodge seemed to embody the classic carol that the choir had sung so beautifully at the Live Nativity. It played in MJ's head still, just after midnight after everyone had gone off to rooms and cabins.

MJ had showered and gotten ready for bed, but she couldn't bear the wait for three a.m. when she climbed under the comforter. So, she bundled into her robe and fuzzy socks and headed downstairs to the lodge kitchen. Telling herself that Christmas breakfast was always a rush, she decided to assemble her ingredients, line up her bowls and mixer and utensils, and maybe sip a cup of chamomile tea.

As she worked, the silence felt reverent in a way, like Christmas Eve had fallen into a hush, holding its breath for morning. Most nights, MJ adored that feeling.

Not tonight or *any* night for the last few weeks. The music had soured her on sleep and she no longer loved that melody or thought this was such a wonderful world.

How could something so small and impossible to explain destroy her sleep and her new relationship and her whole life?

She filled a kettle, staring out at the starry sky and moonlit mountain peaks, her thoughts a million miles away.

When the kettle whistled, she came back to Earth, filled her cup, and bounced a tea bag with small, precise moves that made her feel like this was an important activity.

But it *wasn't* important and she was delaying the inevitable and sickening wake-up call that George sent every night.

Because what else could cause that mysterious music?

"Ridiculous," she whispered, shaking her head as she dropped the soaking tea bag into the trash. "Absolutely ridiculous."

But fear wasn't logical. Grief wasn't logical. And Gracie was right. She had to tell Matt or this would drive a wedge between them that would send him packing by New Year's Day. She could already feel his frustration that he sensed something was wrong—and assumed she didn't reciprocate his feelings.

Nothing could be further from the truth.

But *when* should she tell him? And how do you tell a man you care about that you might be getting messages from beyond the grave telling you to run?

MJ looked up at the sound of footsteps in the hall, only a little surprised when Matt walked into the kitchen. He looked...oh, goodness. Wonderful.

He wore sleep pants and a hoodie, hair damp from

his own late-night shower, looking comfortably handsome.

She felt her heart bloom—that tiny, traitorous ache of longing she'd felt for a year in his absence and constantly in his presence. Didn't George want her to feel that way again?

"Couldn't sleep?" he asked gently.

She tightened her robe. "You know me. Christmas breakfast waits for no one."

He approached the counter, eyeing the small army of ingredients, a knowing smile lifting his lips.

"Two different kinds of cinnamon? Must be Christmas."

She chuckled. "You notice everything."

"I notice you," he said simply.

Her breath caught in her chest. Oh, this man. Why did he have to say things like that with such gentle certainty? Why did it have to feel so...right?

"Want some tea?" she asked, trying to sound casual but failing miserably.

"I'd love some."

She poured the still scalding water from the kettle into a cup and grabbed his favorite herbal tea from the tin display she put out for guests.

Setting a mug before him when he settled at the island, she leaned her hip against the quartz countertop and picked up her own mug, the warmth of the tea seeping into her palms.

The kitchen lights glowed softly off copper pots, the

hush even more pronounced as the two of them stayed perfectly silent.

Matt watched her carefully, as if he could see the thoughts she was trying so hard to hide.

"What's really going on in that beautiful head of yours, MJ?"

Beautiful. When was the last time...

Yesterday, she thought. He'd called her beautiful yesterday and every other day since he'd come back. His compliments were genuine, frequent, and they deserved honesty in return.

For a long second, she stared down at her mug. Steam drifted between them.

She was tired of the secret, the fear, the guilt, the silent middle of the night panic when the opening notes woke her up. It was time.

She exhaled shakily. "All right. There *is* something."

He stayed still, patient, as he always was with her.

"I keep hearing music," she said.

He notched one brow. "What kind of music?"

"A specific song," she said, her throat tightening. "It was very meaningful to...George and me. We always sang it and he had it made into a music box when Gracie was born."

He studied her, deep in thought. "Did the holidays bring this on?" he asked.

"If only it were that simple."

He sipped his tea. "Go ahead," he prompted after he swallowed and she hadn't elaborated.

"It's every night," she continued, words tumbling out.

"At exactly three a.m. I wake up to the melody playing. At first, I thought it was the music box. I tore my apartment apart trying to figure it out. But it wasn't that—Gracie has the music box in her bedroom. So I..." She shook her head. "Matt, I don't know how else to explain it."

He didn't laugh. He didn't scoff. He didn't do anything except lean a little closer, like he understood how delicate this was for her.

"And you think it's George," he guessed.

The fact that he went right there nearly melted her. It was so beautifully intuitive and, somehow, kind. At least it struck her that way.

"I do," she confessed. "I think he's trying to tell me..."

"Not to forget him," he finished. "By being with me."

She just stared at him, because what could she add? That was *exactly* what she thought.

"I'm scared, Matt," she admitted, realizing it was the first time she'd said that out loud. She'd been annoyed, confused, concerned, frustrated, and worried.

But only now did she realize that the music scared her.

"I'm afraid that I'm hurting him or he knows something I don't or that...this isn't right. I don't know," she continued breathlessly. "I know that's crazy, but..."

He shook his head. "Not crazy at all. When did it start?"

"The very night you came back."

His brows lifted. "Never heard it before?"

"No. Not down here." She thumbed in the direction

of the Starling Room, the wedding space that a year ago had been her living quarters. "When construction started, I lived in one of the cabins for a while, but heard nothing. I moved into the upstairs owner's apartment a few months ago, and never heard a thing. Then, the very night you got here, I was awakened at three a.m. by... music."

"What song?"

"*What a Wonderful World.*"

His entire face softened. "No wonder you bolted from that house when we saw the poster."

She laughed softly. "Is there any detail that ever gets by you?"

"Not where you're concerned," he said. "When are you going to figure that out, Mary Jane?"

She reached over the counter and put a hand on his. "You have no idea how much I appreciate that."

He let out a slow breath as he clasped her fingers, his gaze distant as he considered all the possibilities behind this ghostly mystery.

"You loved George," he said, as if it were fact number one. "And you might think that falling in love with another man is somehow deeply disrespectful to him."

Did she? She wasn't sure. "How does that explain the music?"

"Could you be...don't take this the wrong way, but are you—"

"Imagining it?" she supplied with a scoff. "I wish it were that simple, but no, I'm hearing it."

"Okay," he said quickly. "Then maybe there's a logical explanation."

"Other than George himself?"

He angled his head, truly considering that possibility, which she appreciated so much.

"From what you—and others—have told me, it doesn't sound like George was jealous or small or less than loving in life," he said. "So why would he be in death?"

"Oh, Matt. Yes. That's true."

Slowly, he slid off the seat and came around the island, reaching to embrace her with his strong and loving arms.

"Now I know why you're exhausted," he said, pressing his lips to her hair. "You haven't been sleeping. Your grief is rising up at the same time I'm tempting you to fall in love again. It's a lot for anyone, especially someone who carries everyone else's burdens with joy."

She felt her whole body relax into him, so grateful that he understood. She dropped her head back and smiled up at him. "I heard all that, but I kind of drifted off at the part where you said something about falling in love."

Laughing, he kissed her lightly. "I'm a straight shooter, Mary Jane. You know why I'm here and where I hope this is going."

She searched his face, losing herself in his tender brown gaze. "I'm afraid that as long as I'm hearing this music, we aren't going to get there."

He brushed his thumb lightly across her cheek. "Not

if I have anything to say about it. We shall solve the problem together. Three a.m., you say?"

"On the nose, every night, with military precision."

"Then let me stay on your sofa tonight. When the music plays, I'll hear it, too, and help you find the source or figure out where it's coming from."

Her breath hitched. "You'd really do that? On Christmas Eve?"

"Nowhere I'd rather be than near you, helping you, and solving all your problems."

She hugged him tighter, a little overwhelmed with emotion.

"Okay," she whispered. "Yes. Please."

It was nearly one when they finished their tea, shut off the kitchen lights, and headed up to the third floor to her nine-hundred-square-foot one-bedroom apartment.

Just inside, he stopped and sucked in a soft breath.

"What?" she asked. "Do you...feel something?"

"Yeah. Joy, peace, and contentment." He looked around the living area, taking in the small tree by the window, the comfortable sectional with a few throw blankets, the overstuffed chair by the fireplace where she loved to sip tea. "I've never been up here before."

"Well, this is my little home. Far more humble than the ones you're looking at."

"Humble and...perfect, MJ." He took a few steps into the room, first gazing out the picture window that looked out over the mountains. It was dark, but the snowy peaks were awash in the yellow light of a full moon. "It's so cozy and comfortable."

"Well, no media room or walk-in closet or any of the other bells and whistles your real estate agent loves so much."

"My real estate agent, but not me." He paused at a bookshelf, scanning her collection of cookbooks, novels, and a few self-help books on grief.

She watched him take it all in, glancing at her kitchenette with a table for two tucked into the corner. It was all she needed with the glorious kitchen she now had downstairs.

Wandering to the other side, he peeked into her bedroom. The nightlight illuminated her bed, the nightstand with water and some framed pictures, her dresser with a jewelry box and some personal items.

It all felt very intimate for him to see, but he didn't go into the room. Instead, he kissed her on the nose.

"Go get some sleep, beautiful. Grab me a pillow and blanket and let me start a fire and I'll be right there." He gestured toward the sofa in the living room. "Listening."

After she got him squared away, she slipped into her bedroom but left the door open. She crawled under the covers, and let her tired eyes flutter closed. For the first time in weeks, her chest didn't feel tight with dread.

As she drifted toward sleep, she could hear the faint creak of the sofa as he turned over, then a soft sigh and the rustle of his pillowcase.

His presence filled the little apartment with a sense of safety she hadn't realized she'd been craving.

"I'm sorry, George," she mouthed in the dark, tears stinging. "I love him."

No one answered, but she folded the admission into her heart and finally fell asleep.

THE SOUND YANKED her awake like an insistent hand shaking her shoulder.

The familiar melody played—well, beeped—in its usual muffled way, as if someone were playing it through a pillow, but distinct enough that her heart did that awful, familiar lurch.

MJ blinked into the dark, disoriented for a few seconds by the fact that she didn't feel alone. The apartment wasn't empty.

The living room lights came on—all of them, including the overheads—but she didn't move yet. She stayed long enough to hear the music play through the second of four measures of the familiar song, gentle and maddeningly exact in its timing.

She swallowed hard, then pushed herself upright. Her legs were heavy with sleep, but her nerves snapped awake. She slipped on her robe and tiptoed barefoot out of the bedroom.

Matt was already up, still in his hoodie and sleep pants, hair rumpled, moving around the space like a focused bloodhound. He had one cushion off the sofa, his head cocked as he listened to the music.

Relief almost buckled her knees.

"You hear it," she whispered.

He turned, his eyes clear and awake. "Loud and clear."

"Actually, soft and muted."

"True..." He stood perfectly still and narrowed his eyes, turning slowly...slowly...trying to follow the sound as she had so, so many times.

"It'll stop in a second," she said. "Four times through the melody."

"Then I need to move quickly." He walked toward the fireplace, leaning down as if he were listening to the actual floorboards. "Do any of these come up? Secret hiding place?"

"Not that I know of, but honestly? I've never checked."

"You test the floorboards and I will..." He got closer to the fireplace. "Is this new?" he asked, indicating the mantel and stone around it.

"Everything is new. The space was here, but it was an unfinished attic that my grandfather once used as a workshop. We gutted it and transformed it into this apartment."

He nodded, leaning toward the fireplace. "It's coming from over here."

She couldn't disagree—it did sound like that part of the room. Giving up on the floorboards, she followed him, her robe pulled tight around her like armor.

"Right here," he said, tapping the drywall next to the fireplace stone. He stepped to the wall, ear and palm hovering close like he was scanning for a hidden safe. "I feel something! Vibrations or—oh."

The music stopped.

"That's it?" he asked, genuinely disappointed.

"Until three a.m. tomorrow," she said. "Then he'll—I mean *it*—will be back."

He stepped back to look up and down the wall and the fireplace mantel. "What was in this spot before the remodel?"

She frowned, trying to picture the workroom. It was so different then, and she'd spent very little time up here, using the space mostly for storage.

"I think that's where Grandpa Owen kept a worktable."

"Anything electric?"

She frowned. "What do you mean?"

"Right before it stopped, I felt the slightest vibration in the wall. Something is back there making the sound. I know it's not your music box, but something like that, only it doesn't sound...mechanical. Does that make sense?"

Nothing made sense. "Maybe," she conceded. "But why would it start two weeks ago and always play at a specific time?"

"I don't know, but I could find out if..." He angled his head toward the wall. "I could do a little demolition. I'll be neat and have it fixed in a day, I promise."

She lifted a shoulder. "You can try, but there's nothing in the wall but insulation and ancient lodge dust and probably a couple of spiders."

He gave her a look that said *trust me.* "Can I cut a hole in the drywall?"

"Now?"

"Can't think of a better time."

She gave a breathy laugh. "Matt Walker, at three in the morning on Christmas Eve, you want to do surgery on my apartment because..."

He took a step closer and put his hands on her shoulders, drawing her into him. "Because I want to eliminate the possibility of the late, great George McBride keeping me from spending the rest of my life loving you."

"Oh." She put her fingers over her mouth, the sentiment so sweet.

"So, Mary Jane, if you'll let me cut a hole, we can settle the sound. If it's him, I'll back away. If it's not, well...life as you know it is about to change for the better."

She wasn't sure what that meant—move into one of those big houses? Well, now wasn't the time to discuss that. Now was the time to answer her questions.

"Then get some tools from the mudroom, Graham Matthew Walker. You know, the red toolbox from when you saved me from a plumbing emergency."

"I know the box well. Gimme a sec."

When Matt returned, he carried a small handsaw with a pointed tip and a short, jagged blade that she recognized from her tool collection.

"You have the perfect jab saw," he told her, holding it up. "This'll cut clean without destroying the whole wall. This place is too special to hurt."

"Thank you." She stood back to observe the process.

He pressed the sharp tip into the drywall with

controlled force until it punctured. Then he sawed a careful square, the blade rasping softly. Drywall dust drifted to the floor like pale snow. MJ watched with a weird combination of dread and fascination, clutching her robe.

Finally, he pried the little square of drywall free, grabbed his phone from the coffee table, and used the flashlight to peer in.

"What do you see?" MJ asked, not surprised that she was holding her breath.

"I see..." His shoulders moved like he was... laughing.

"What is it?"

With a smirk, he handed her the light and stepped back, allowing her a chance to look into the open space behind the wall, right next to the firebox. There, resting on a wood beam, was a cell phone plugged into a charger that ran to a loose electrical box.

MJ slapped a hand over her mouth. "What the heck?"

"Let me see if I can reach it," he said, easing her to the side to stick his arm all the way in. Making a face, he stretched and stretched, then slowly pulled his arm out, an iPhone dangling from a cord.

"How did that get in there?"

"Probably a construction worker who forgot it," Matt said, touching the screen to bring it to life. Sliding his finger over the glass, he tapped the clock app, went to alarms, and there it was.

Daily Wake Up 3:00 AM What a Wonderful World

MJ let out a sound that was half gasp, half strangled laugh. "That's...an alarm."

"Yep."

"In my wall."

"Also yep." He tugged the cord. "It's been plugged in this whole time."

"Who on Earth—"

Matt followed the cord to the outlet. He tugged lightly, then frowned in concentration. "The charger's plugged into an interior electrical socket. That socket must be live but wasn't before, or it wouldn't have passed code. Have you had any electrical work done recently?"

MJ felt her jaw open. "Jack had electricians at the lodge the morning of their wedding! One of the speakers in the Starling Room was wonky and they had to do something to the circuit breaker."

"They most likely brought this old outlet to life and—wham—you're getting some poor guy's three o'clock wake-up call." He tapped a few times and brought the phone's home screen up, showing a picture of a muscular man with a baby on his knee.

"Oh! That's...Izzy! He built the fireplace. He told me he drove all the way from Ogden and had to get up at three to get to the gym and make it here by seven. And that's his baby...little Ashton." She smiled, remembering the kind young man who her contractor said was one of the best stone masons in Utah.

"So he accidentally left his phone charging and you never heard it because they closed up the wall—"

"Goodness, yes. They finished the drywall when Izzy

was out for a few days. They must have missed the phone and the socket went dead...until the electrician activated the line."

"The phone came back to life," he finished. "Izzy's alarm started going off again."

MJ blinked as the puzzle pieces fell into place and the picture was...not scary or supernatural or confusing. It all made sense.

Matt chuckled at the look on her face. "Do you have a way to reach Izzy to tell him you have his phone?"

"I'll call the contractor," she said, shaking her head as a wave of warm relief washed over her.

"So the mystery is solved," Matt said, a slow smile lifting his lips. "Do you feel better?"

She sighed. "Yes, I do. Thank you, Matt." She wiped at her eyes, surprised to find they had tears in them. "I feel like I can breathe again," she confessed.

Putting the phone down, he wrapped her in a tight hug. "Honey, I didn't know your wonderful husband, but I do have this much in common with him—he loved you, and so do I."

MJ felt a little wobbly. "Oh, Matt."

She pulled back and looked at him in the bright living room lights, seeing everything so clearly now.

"George wouldn't have wanted me to be scared," she said quietly. "He wouldn't have wanted me lonely. I know that."

Matt's eyes were steady on hers. "I think he'd want you happy."

"I think so, too." Her voice shook. "And I think he'd like you."

Matt smiled. "High praise. Thank you."

MJ reached up and touched his face, letting the truth rise without fighting it. "I love you."

His breath caught, like the words hit someplace deep. Just as he lowered his head to kiss her, they heard a loud, high-pitched scream that cut through the hushed night.

MJ gasped. "What was that?"

They both rushed to the window, looking down to see Cabin Four lit up with every possible light, the front door gaping open.

"Help! Help me!" a woman screamed.

Not any woman—*Bianca*.

That woman could ruin anything—including MJ's best moment in many years.

Without saying a word, they both rushed to the door. MJ grabbed her phone on the way, instinct telling her to call Gracie.

Chapter Seventeen

Gracie

G racie woke to the sound of her phone buzzing against the nightstand, a persistent, vibrating rattle that yanked her straight up through layers of sleep. She blinked at the dark room, disoriented, and fumbled for the phone, squinting at the screen.

Mom

Her stomach dropped. No one called at—what was it, four-thirty?—on Christmas morning unless there was a big, fat problem.

She swiped. "What's wrong?"

MJ's voice came in a breathless whisper. "Bianca's screaming outside. Like—*screaming*. Matt and I are going out now."

Gracie bolted upright. "What? Why?"

"I don't know but she's yelling for help. I thought you'd want to know." MJ hung up before Gracie could say anything else...like why she was with Matt at this hour?

Pushing that thought away, she launched out of bed and grabbed the sweatshirt draped over a chair. She yanked it over her pajama top, found sweats and socks, jumping around the dark room to hastily dress.

Bianca screaming for help outside the lodge? What in the world—

Halfway in her second sock, the fog of sleep cleared in a rush as a horrifying possibility flashed through her mind.

Bigfoot.

They wouldn't have! They couldn't have!

But this was Benny and Red and nothing—not any homemade, wildly misguided, slightly ridiculous, and possibly dangerous escapade—was out of the question.

She could actually hear her son cook up an idea like that.

I know, Grandpa! What if we scare her so bad she leaves Utah forever? Like, Bigfoot-level scare.

"Oh, no. No, no, no—please *no*."

She hurried into the hallway, pausing in the glow of the nightlight that made sure both Benny and Red could find their way to the bathroom in the middle of the night. They slept across the hall from each other, at the end in the back of the rambling old house.

Both of their doors were closed and no light seeped out from under either one.

Could they have snuck out to pretend to be Bigfoot? Again, with this duo, anything was possible.

With a gut-sick feeling, she marched to Red's door, pressing her ear against the wood, hoping to hear his loud and distinctive snore. Nothing. She twisted the knob and flung it open.

Red shot up in bed like he'd been launched from a toaster, his white beard bushy, his eyes cloudy but fearful.

"Who died?" he croaked.

"No one, I hope," Gracie shot back. "Bianca's screaming outside and I need to make sure you're *not* out there pretending to be Bigfoot."

Red blinked. Then blinked again, trying to make sense of the accusation. "Why would I—? Sweet fancy Moses, you don't think Benny..."

"I hope not," she said dryly. "Because you'll both be grounded for a year."

"Me? What did I do?"

"Guilt by association."

They hurried to Benny's room, Red shuffling in his pajamas and thick wool socks. Gracie cracked Benny's door open, bracing herself.

Her little boy was sprawled across the bed, mouth open, drooling on his pillow, breathing in that unmistakably deep, unshakeable sleep of an eleven-year-old who'd spent the evening with sheep, goats, and baby Jesus in the snow.

Gracie let out a shaky breath of relief.

"Okay," she whispered. "Good. Stay here with him. I'll go see what's going on."

Red nodded, still bleary. "Call me if you need an ambulance or a bat to clobber Bigfoot."

"Not funny." She headed toward the stairs, her mind spinning.

If Benny and Red weren't behind whatever Bianca saw, then what could possibly have terrified her in the dark?

She snagged her jacket from the hook by the kitchen

door, stuck her feet in boots, and stepped into the quiet, frigid night.

A thick layer of snow from a few hours ago coated the ground, fresh enough that her boots sank deeply with every step. The air hung blue and breathless, that hour when the world felt unreal and still.

She was halfway to the lodge when a thick cloud covered the moon and she reached for her—

Dang. Her phone was next to her bed. She hurried down the trail toward the cabins, breath puffing white as she imagined what might have unfolded.

Had Bianca run to *him*? Screaming in the middle of the night just to get his attention?

Or—what if Bianca really was pregnant and something had gone wrong? What if she was bleeding or in pain? Of course she'd go to Marshall.

Her breath faltered as she remembered how they'd ended the evening.

She had barely had a chance to talk to Marshall after the Live Nativity. She'd driven home with Red and Benny, who conked out in the van. She had to get him to bed and then returned to get the cabin key for Marshall, who was in Bianca's cabin doing...midnight presents.

The last thing she heard was Bianca begging Marshall to stay and help her put Olivia to bed on Christmas Eve—*just like the old days!*

Marshall, apologetic and visibly uncomfortable, had accepted the key Gracie handed him for Cabin Two and softly promised they'd talk tomorrow.

It was possible Bianca was just drumming up drama

and sympathy and was, right now, in the arms of her ex-husband getting comfort...and setting her evil plans in motion.

The prospect made Gracie's stomach roll—not that she thought Marshall would fall for it. Not a bit. But still...everything about that woman was unsettling.

Gracie cut across the path and rounded the corner toward the cabins. Just as she had Marshall's cabin in sight, she spotted Bianca launching up the stairs to his door.

She pounded on the wood with both fists.

"Marshall!" Bianca shrieked into the silent night. "Help me! There's a bear! Marsh!"

A few seconds later, the door opened and Marshall, sleepy-eyed and wearing only flannel sleep pants, blinked at her. "Bianca? What—"

She launched herself closer. "Please! It's still out here!"

Gracie stayed frozen in the shadows across the path, hidden by a giant pine tree, able to watch and hear them as long as they stayed outside. If they went in together, well, then, all bets were off.

Bianca wrapped herself around Marshall, still shrieking about a bear. Gracie could hear him mutter something and Bianca actually laughed—another inside joke? Another memory?

Whatever it was, the exchange was enough for him to back inside and—oh, *no*. Bianca followed, obviously invited.

No! Was he that dumb, desperate, or dense? Didn't he see what she was up to?

For an instant, Gracie considered telling him—right now. She should just storm up there, pound on the door, demand Bianca come clean, force the issue out into the open, and...and...and look entirely unhinged.

No. She had to trust him. Alone with his warm and willing ex-wife, who'd come to Park City for the sole purpose of seducing him. Her plan could never work—Marshall wasn't dumb.

But he had a soft, good heart and that's what Bianca was counting on.

Gracie took a deep, painful breath, turned, and walked away. She put one foot in front of the other and found herself on the long wooded trail that snaked through the woods.

It would get her home—the long way.

That was fine, because she needed a minute to breathe, to think, to keep herself from falling apart in the snow. Was Marshall not the man she'd hoped he'd be—the man she'd started to believe he was?

Certainly not a man who'd take what Bianca was offering, but then...he was a man. Flawed, human, and tender-hearted.

Her boots crunched softly. The world was quiet again until she heard a rustle in the distance, and a thump, and a...*breath*?

Gracie froze.

A twig cracked and some leaves crunched. Then she heard the unmistakable sound of heavy footsteps and more labored breaths. Her heart leapt into her throat as it got closer and closer.

She threw a look over her shoulder just in time to catch a massive silhouette emerging from the trees. Huge, hulking, and covered in shaggy fur. That was either Benny or a bear or...

"Bigfoot," she croaked the word as she started to run, her boots slipping wildly on the snowy incline.

She stumbled, slid, and pitched sideways into a deep drift, snow exploding around her as cold crystals rushed over her coat and into her hood.

Footsteps pounded behind her. The breathing got louder.

She covered her head with both arms, squeezed her eyes shut, and prayed she wouldn't get mauled and murdered on Christmas Eve in the woods.

A hand grabbed her shoulder.

She opened her mouth and sucked in a breath to let out a blood-curdling—

"Gracie?" a familiar voice said. "For heaven's sake, honey. It's me. Bertie."

She cracked one eye open.

Bertie Kessler stood over her, bundled in a monstrous puffer jacket, enormous fur hat perched on her head. Her breath puffed steadily, as if she'd been out walking for hours.

"Oh, my gosh." Gracie sagged into the snow. "Bertie! You scared me half to death."

"Well, you look half dead," Bertie said matter-of-factly, offering her a hand. "Get up. You're going to freeze in that snow pile."

Gracie managed to get to her feet. Snow cascaded off her coat and down her legs. "Why are you out here? It's almost four in the morning."

"Oh, I can't sleep past three, sometimes four if I'm lucky," Bertie huffed. "So I get my steps in. Body burns best in a fasted state. Ask Red. I taught him that."

Gracie let out a slightly off-key little laugh. "Did you...did you see anything strange? Like...a bear?"

"Only strange thing out here is you acting like you're being kidnapped." Bertie clicked her tongue. "I saw Bianca running down the lodge road earlier. Thought she was having some sort of fit."

That's what Bianca saw—the octogenarian cardio queen power-walking in a fur hat that could camouflage a moose.

Well, at least Bianca had been legitimately terrified. She wasn't losing a pregnancy.

She'd simply been given a great excuse to run straight into Marshall's cabin—and arms.

"Now, you get yourself home, Gracie," Bertie said with authority. "It's Christmas morning and you have a young child."

She was right. Adrenaline dumping hard, Gracie said goodbye and headed toward the main lodge road, needing to get out of the woods. She didn't want to pass Cabin Two again—but it was much faster and safer that way. The curved path forced her right past the front porch... where light spilled from the open doorway.

He'd left the door open—that was encouraging. He would risk freezing rather than be alone with Bianca.

Voices drifted into the night, both strained, then she spotted their silhouettes in the doorway.

Gracie moved carefully behind a clump of shrubs and pines, hidden in shadow again. How many times had she reprimanded Benny for eavesdropping on conversations?

Many. At least he came by it honestly, since she had no intention of *not* listening to this.

She stayed perfectly still and narrowed her eyes to concentrate on hearing the words that floated through the chilly night. Whatever they were saying, she was invested enough in Marshall that she had to know. She *had* to.

Bianca stood in the open doorway, arms folded tight across her chest, her breath fogging in angry bursts.

Marshall stood just inside, still barefoot but he'd pulled on a sweatshirt. Even from here, he looked braced, his shoulders tense.

"...just hear me out," Bianca pleaded. "I know I made mistakes. I know I wasn't perfect. I know I—I messed things up. But things can be different now."

Marshall exhaled, patient but wary. "Bianca..."

"No, Marshall, please." She stepped closer, sounding desperate. "Olivia deserves both her parents under the same roof. Don't you think she does? Don't you think she misses that? Don't you think she *needs* that?"

Gracie's heart twisted painfully. Playing the Olivia card was just not fair. Everyone knew that child was

Marshall's weakness. He'd do anything to protect and love her.

"I love you, Marsh," she continued, undaunted by Marshall's lack of response. Or maybe encouraged by it— he wasn't telling her *no* or *please leave* or *we shouldn't even be talking*.

He just stood, strong and stone silent.

Gracie dug deep into her soul and tried to decide how to feel about that. Trusting. She wanted to trust him. If she was ready to fall in love with the guy, she had to trust him. Starting right this minute.

"I never stopped loving you!" Bianca wailed. "The divorce was a huge mistake. My choices were...can we just say it? Stupid! Foolish! Doesn't everyone deserve a second chance? Especially the mother of your daughter! The woman you swore to honor and cherish till death do we part?"

But she'd cheated on him!

Gracie bit back her response, blood pumping as hard as it had when she thought Bigfoot was on her tail.

"I'm so serious, Marshall. I'm yours. I love you. I'll never hurt you again." The sincerity and crack in her voice—fake or not—was powerful. Bianca rarely sounded vulnerable, but she did now. "I will even go to church with you, Marsh! Like you always asked. I will. I promise!"

Whoa, she was pulling out all the stops now. And how would he react?

A long moment passed and Gracie held her breath.

"Bianca." Marshall stepped all the way outside,

easing Bianca further out onto the porch. "Listen to me." His voice was quiet, steady, and just forceful enough that Gracie could listen, too.

"What, honey? Anything."

"Nothing you say or do will change my mind," he said. "You are Olivia's biological mother, and, for that reason, you will be in the outer space of my life as long as she is, which will be forever."

"Outer space?" Bianca choked. "What does that mean?"

"That means I don't want you close to me."

Gracie let out a stunned exhale.

"Olivia and I are happy here. We're building a life. And I've met someone very, very special."

The blood thumped too hard in Gracie's ears for her to hear Bianca's response—but she didn't need to. What she said didn't matter. But Marshall? *That* mattered.

"The truth is," he continued. "I'm falling in love."

Gracie's knees nearly buckled. She grabbed a nearby branch for balance and felt tears sting her eyes while a clump of snow meandered down her wrist, icy and frozen.

"In love?" Bianca sputtered. "With...with that redheaded bakery girl?"

Gracie fought a laugh that she heard Marshall let out.

"If you mean Gracie McBride, yes," he said, his voice warm and proud.

"She's not in your league," Bianca scoffed.

"She's way beyond it," he fired back.

"What could you possibly see in her? She's scared of

her own shadow, blushes if you look sideways, and never fights for you. Have you noticed?"

He laughed again. "Have I noticed that she's classy, sensitive, and puts other people first? Yes." He paused, emotion thickening his voice. "I've noticed that she's an incredible mother and a successful business owner and a loving daughter and…and…beautiful inside and out."

Gracie didn't know whether to faint with happiness or hold still and listen to the next heartfelt compliment. He really saw her like that?

"And I plan to spend the rest of my life with her," he said, his sweet words floating on the cold air right into her heart. "She just doesn't know it yet."

She absolutely couldn't breathe.

"By this time next year, I hope we'll be engaged if not already married."

A tiny, involuntary sound escaped Gracie's throat as she stumbled backwards, a twig snapping under her boot.

Bianca shrieked and jumped behind Marshall. "It's the bear! It's back!"

Marshall gently peeled her off. "Bianca. There is no bear."

He frowned and peered into the darkness, where Gracie froze, lungs locked.

If he saw her here—eavesdropping—she'd die on the spot. So much for classy and beautiful. How about meddlesome and insecure?

Gracie stayed rooted in the shadows, silent and still.

Bianca stomped her foot. "You can't do this to me!" she cried. "I need you! I'm pregnant!"

Marshall jerked backwards. "What?"

"I am but I want you to be the father!"

He choked a laugh. "Well, I'm not and you know it." He shook his head. "At least now I know your secret agenda."

"It could work, Marshall. It could—"

"No, Bianca. You need someone else, but it's not me. It'll never be me. But I'm praying for you and will always be there if you need something, but it won't be my life or heart. Is that clear?"

Red was right! Gracie pressed her hand to her chest, watching Bianca take a few steps backwards and hold up her hands in surrender.

"You know what? You're right. I should go. In fact, I should leave altogether."

He didn't argue.

"Yep, I'm done. *Done.* I don't need to be here for Christmas morning. Olivia doesn't care. It's all Benny and Gracie and all these dumb mountain people who live in the snow! I'll Uber to the airport in the morning. Enjoy the bears! Hope one doesn't get me on the way back!"

With that, she spun and marched down the lodge road toward her cabin, grumbling under her breath.

Marshall watched her go, shoulders sagging a little. Then he reached up and rubbed the back of his neck, sighing into the cold. Finally, he retreated into the cabin and closed the door, the light going out instantly.

Gracie stood perfectly still until Bianca disappeared around the bend, then another full minute just to let all his beautiful words replay in her mind.

Classy...sensitive...successful...incredible. And her personal favorite: *I plan to spend the rest of my life with her...she just doesn't know it yet.*

Well, she knew it now. And what would a shy, introverted, slightly-overwhelmed-by-life girl *do* with that information? Sleep on it? Share it with her mother and cousin? Or...

She stepped out from behind the tree, her heart thundering as she carefully walked directly to the cabin. She climbed the two steps and stood in front of the door, hand raised, ready to knock.

She knew one thing—if she did this, she'd never go back. This was do or die. Life with Marshall Hampton would begin right now at dawn on Christmas morning and they—

The door whipped open. "I told you to—"

Gracie launched herself forward and kissed him. She grabbed his head, held him steady, and gave every ounce of pent-up love and longing and hope into one toe-curling, soul-stealing, life-changing kiss.

When she broke away, breathless and snow-dusted, she whispered, "This time next year?"

"You were listening," he said, chuckling into another kiss.

"Yes, sir, I was. I'm the bear who heard every word."

He drew back, his brows lifting. "And?"

"And I like the way you think, Marshall Hampton."

He pulled her into his arms and kissed her again as the snow whispered softly around them and Christmas morning crept quietly into the mountains.

Chapter Eighteen

Elise

The handicapped van always smelled faintly like vinyl and peppermint gum, thanks to her father's lifelong Altoids habit. Elise sat belted into the passenger-side wheelchair station, her gloved hands resting on the padded armrests, breathing in the familiar scent and wishing that she didn't feel like *cargo*.

She didn't usually feel that way, but last night's conversation with Wade hung over her mood, darkening it.

Dad drove carefully through the fresh Christmas morning snow, windshield wipers brushing away flurries that looked like rising sparks. Mom sat in the front holding a casserole dish, and all around, the van was piled with gifts. Everything felt warm and bright and festive except for Elise, who could not seem to unclench her jaw.

Her mother turned. "Sweetheart, you're awfully quiet."

"I'm fine," Elise said instantly, plastering on a smile.

"You didn't sleep well?" she pressed.

"Who sleeps well on Christmas Eve?" Elise quipped. "Santa anxiety is real."

"Elise." The tone was both gentle and knowing.

Elise exhaled slowly, her mind going back to last night.

He hadn't meant to hurt her. Wade Reynolds was kind down to the marrow. But when he'd gone on a *mobility science* rant, her heart had stumbled over every word.

Her mother let the silence stretch a little, then asked softly, "Did something happen with Wade?"

"No," Elise said quickly. "Of course not. We're just... friends. He helped with Shambles and the Nativity thing last night. That's all."

He also stole my heart, gave me my first kiss, and made me think about a future I never dreamed I could have.

She kept all that to herself.

"He's a sweetheart," Mom said, still turned to look at Elise. "And he clearly cares about you."

"He cares about *everything*," Elise said, sharper than intended. "That's exactly the issue."

Her mother didn't press again, so it was quiet except for Bing Crosby crooning about a *White Christmas*, which her father put on repeat until they reached Snowberry Lodge.

There, Dad pulled around back to the kitchen door because it was the only entrance without stairs and how Elise always got in and out of the lodge.

Her whole body prickled as she unclipped her chest strap, braced as her dad lowered the van's lift, and rolled into the crisp Christmas air. The tension was understandable, since she was minutes from seeing Wade.

Inside the kitchen, warmth wrapped around Elise

instantly. Cinnamon rolls baked in the oven, pine-scented candles flickered, and a familiar chorus of Starling, Kessler and McBride voices drifted from the great room.

"Elise!" MJ swept over, hugging her lightly and avoiding bumping the chair. "Merry Christmas."

"And to you, Aunt MJ!" Elise grinned. "Nic texted me this morning. I heard you and Matt made a huge discovery last night."

The older woman flushed. "I thought I had ghosts. Turned out I had the phone of a construction worker."

They laughed about that, then she moved with her parents to the great room and set their gifts beneath the tree. A bunch of conversations overlapped, while Newt bounded through the room wearing a big red ribbon and bow as a collar. She hugged and helloed, and tried not to spin her chair in every direction looking for the man who was not in the room.

Not surprising. He was a lodge guest, not family, and not obligated to attend the festivities.

Disappointment went to war with relief, and—oddly enough—relief won. She didn't have to look him in the eye and pretend she wasn't stung, rattled, and cracked wide open.

"Elise!" Nicole swung down beside her and plopped onto the sofa. "Merry Christmas, lady!"

"Merry Christmas. You look like you swallowed a secret."

Nicole flashed a guilty smile. "Me? *Nooo.*" Her knee bounced. "Okay, maybe a tiny one."

"Where's Cameron?" Elise asked.

"Uh... around." Nicole picked up her phone and gave a soft gasp as she read the screen. "Okay, then. Let's take a walk."

"A walk? Now? Where are we going?"

"Stop interrogating and show me why you're called Hale on Wheels." She gestured toward the kitchen. "Chop-chop, sister."

Elise followed, more curious with every passing second. On the way, Nicole grabbed a jacket and tossed Elise her fur poncho from where she'd left it in the mudroom.

"We're going outside?" Elise asked.

"Do the words *Christmas surprise* mean nothing to you?" Nicole quipped.

They crossed the plowed path to the stables, breath visible in the crisp air. At the big door, Nicole paused dramatically.

"Are you ready?" she asked.

"I'm actually not sure."

With her fiftieth sly smile, Nicole pushed open the stable door, letting in a rectangle of bright, icy sunlight.

"Elise," she said softly. "Go on."

Elise rolled forward on instinct, expecting...honestly, she had no idea what to expect.

What she *didn't* expect was Wade.

He stood in the center of the stable beside Cameron, both of them flanking Copper's stall. But that wasn't what made Elise's breath catch.

It was the ramp.

An enormous, gleaming, mechanized wheelchair ramp sat in front of Copper's stall. It was...beautiful—hydraulic, adjustable, and electric. A veritable wheelchair elevator made to rise straight up to a horse.

Beside it was a custom saddle rig with a harness configuration unlike anything she'd ever seen outside a therapy barn.

Copper, curious and calm, poked his nose over the stall door as if to say, *Well? Look what they did.*

Wade lifted his gaze slowly.

He looked tentative, as if he had no idea whether this would heal her or shatter her.

"Elise," he said, voice steady but soft. "Merry Christmas."

Her heart punched against her ribs.

For a beat, she couldn't speak or breathe. Tears pricked her eyes and she blinked them away furiously.

Nicole touched her shoulder. "This is why I was weird," she whispered. "Cam helped him set it up. It arrived at sunrise."

Cameron grinned. "The instructions were terrible, but we figured it out."

Elise swallowed hard. The cold air from outside clashed with the sudden heat in her chest.

Wade took a barely perceptible step forward. "It's a... ramp."

Her laugh escaped on a shaky breath. "I see that."

"And a new saddle."

"Yes, that, too."

"And a harness configuration that'll let you ride

Copper without anyone helping you up or trailing you around the paddock."

Her fingers tightened around the wheels of her chair. "Wade..."

He inhaled slowly. "I know how things sounded last night," he said. "And I know this might feel like more of the same. But it isn't. Elise...this isn't about fixing you."

The words struck like a bell, vibrating through her.

He hesitated before glancing at Cam and Nicole. "Can we talk? Just the two of us?"

Cam squeezed her shoulder. "We'll be inside, E. Take your time."

When they left, Wade's expression grew serious. "I owe you an explanation before you accept this gift. May I offer you a ride?"

Right then, he could have asked for anything—the moon, a million dollars, her undying love. The answer would have been yes.

She just looked at him and nodded, feeling hot and oddly light, as if someone had reduced the gravity in the room. Wade's green eyes held hers, bright and earnest beneath the brim of that black cowboy hat.

"Let me show you," he said quietly. "And if you hate it, we shut it down, we take it apart, I'll haul every piece off this property myself. Deal?"

Her heart hammered as she rolled closer. The unit was sleek and solid, bolted securely on a platform on the floor. The whole thing was edged with low safety rails, and looked like it was operated by a control panel mounted at arm height. On the far side, a wide, padded gate lined up perfectly with Copper's girth as Wade opened the stall door and led him out.

"It works a lot like the van lift," Wade said, keeping his voice low, giving her space to take it all in. "You roll on, lock your chair, hit the button to raise the platform. Once you're level with the saddle, you've got this transfer bar here." He tapped a sturdy, swiveling arm attached to the side. "You grab, pivot, and lower yourself over. The saddle's got side blocks and this discreet hip strap once you're settled. It can all be done on your own."

Elise studied each part, her brain automatically assessing angles, distances, failure points. "And if Copper moves?"

"I'll hold him for the demo. And later, if you want to work up to doing the whole thing alone, you can. This rig's rated for unassisted use. Auburn's been using a similar design for years with their equine therapy program. I called in a bunch of favors to get this here in time. So, uh... if you could pretend to like it, that'd be great for my ego."

She huffed out a laugh in spite of herself. "You called Auburn?"

"I sweet-talked half of Alabama and UPS," he said. "Christmas miracles all around."

The flutters in her stomach intensified. Part of her wanted to bolt. Part of her wanted to launch herself onto that horse and never come down. And part of her wanted to throw her arms around Wade Reynolds and kiss him senseless.

"Okay," she said, hearing the tremor in her voice and deciding not to care. "Show me."

Wade stepped behind her chair and gave a gentle push to line her up with the platform. "Straight on," he murmured. "That's it. A little more...yes. Perfect. Lock your brakes."

His hands brushed hers as she set the brakes, sending a shiver up her arms.

"Ready?" he asked.

No, not even close. "Yes."

"Press this button," he said, indicating a lighted panel.

She did and the lift hummed, smooth and steady, raising slowly her until she was level with Copper's withers. From this vantage point, she could see the top of the horse's back, the gleam of the new leather saddle rig.

The saddle had soft extra padding at the thighs, with a slightly deeper seat that would hold her more securely than a standard style. She noticed a curved, thick handle built into the front horn—not obvious, but practical and reassuring.

Straps along the side could fasten around her hips and thighs, keeping her secure without looking like she was being attached to the contraption.

Copper flicked an ear back toward her and snorted softly.

"Hey, handsome," Elise murmured, reaching out to scratch his neck. "You're in on this scheme, huh?"

"He's been very patient," Wade said with a smile, a

hand on Copper's halter. "We did a couple test runs so he wouldn't freak. He's good to go."

She studied the space between her body and the saddle. She'd done transfers a thousand times—bed, chair, car, exam tables. This was the same process, just a little higher, a little scarier, and with a large, breathing animal attached.

But no one had to carry or hold her.

Fear nipped at the edges of her bravado. Before the accident, riding had been freedom. After, it had become... abject sadness. Until Nicole and Copper, she'd given up completely.

Since then, she'd gotten used to two people lifting her, someone pushing her, escorting her, *babysitting* her. Grateful as she was, it always felt like borrowing freedom instead of owning it.

She tightened her grip on the bar, set her jaw, and shifted her weight.

"Easy," Wade murmured, his hands hovering near her waist, not touching unless she needed him. "Strong transfer, just like you do with your shower and bed. You can do this, Elise."

He'd never seen her do any of those transfers, but the fact that he knew she did and respected the work involved meant a lot to her.

Taking a steadying inhale, she pivoted on her chair cushion, lifted with her arms and shoulders, slid across. For a breathless second, her center of gravity wobbled and the world tilted—but then the saddle caught her. Wade's hand stayed close, but not on her.

In her next breath, she was seated, centered, and she'd done it alone!

Wade made a sound that was almost a laugh and a groan together. "You are incredible," he said, his voice thick.

"Don't you forget it," she replied, but her eyes stung as she reached down to fasten the low-profile hip strap, securing herself to the saddle.

"That's mostly for the unexpected," he explained as he watched her work. "Spooks, little slips. You've got good core strength. I wanted something that gives you an extra second to grab a hold if needed."

She glanced down. Her boots rested in the low stirrups more for appearance than function, but it felt...right, somehow. Her flowing burgundy skirt split easily but still covered everything. It would be even better in riding clothes. But the skirt made her feel pretty.

The lift platform lowered back to the floor with her empty chair in place. Copper shifted one step, and Elise's body moved with him. She sucked in a breath. It was like a missing piece sliding into place.

She picked up the reins and gave a snap to Copper, who started to walk toward the stable doors.

Wade hustled ahead and opened them, clearing the way to the snow-covered ring. The air was cold but not brutal, her breath fogging in front of her. Copper's hooves thudded softly on the packed ground.

She circled once at a walk, holding the reins, getting used to the feel of this new rig. The saddle held her firmly, but not rigidly. She felt secure and yet strangely... unbound.

Best of all, Wade was forty feet away. She was riding *alone*!

"This is amazing," she said, the words escaping on a laugh. "I can't even feel how the saddle is attached, just that I'm not going anywhere."

"That's the idea," Wade said, leaning against the very same railing where she'd first spotted him a few weeks ago.

The paddock fell quiet except for Copper's breathing and the occasional swoosh of his tail. Snowflakes drifted lazily out of a sky the color of soft pewter.

Wade stayed where he was, so she walked the horse to the railing, stopping to look down at him from the saddle.

"Well," she said, shifting the reins through her fingers. "You went big."

He pushed up to perch on the top rail, just about eye to eye with her. "Can I tell you a story about my dog named Murphy?"

She blinked. "Your...dog?"

"Yeah." He slipped a boot onto the lower rung of the rail. His hat shadowed his eyes, but she could see the nerves in the way he wrapped his bare hands around the wood of the top rail. "Can I tell it without you making fun of my 'bama accent? Because I may lean into it."

"I never make fun of your accent," she said, then ruined it by adding, "Not to your face."

He huffed a laugh. "Fair. Okay." He drew in a breath

that looked like it hurt a little. "When I was fifteen, I had a dog I loved so much, an Irish setter named Murphy. He got bone cancer."

She felt her lip go out in pity. "Sadness."

"He started limping one day and they found it. And you know, the vet told my dad all the practical things. The cost of surgery, the rough recovery, the crappy odds. It made sense, on paper, to let him go."

She let out a sympathetic whimper, rubbing her hands together but forgetting the cold.

"I remember I just sat on the kitchen floor with that dog's head in my lap and realized that Murph didn't know anything about money or odds or spreadsheets. He just knew how to be my best pal. But we were going to put him down to spare *us* the hard part. And I—I couldn't live with that."

"You weren't an oncologist yet," she said softly, rapt. "What did you do?"

"I put my little dial-up modem to work and went to war with every article, every printout, every late-night forum post about three-legged dogs. I told my parents if they said yes to the surgery, I'd handle the rest. The lifting, the icing, the meds, the ramp off the porch, since he couldn't do stairs. I begged them for a chance to fight for Murphy's good days instead of just...folding in front of the bad ones."

He waited a beat and smiled, holding her gaze, looking so sweet and smart and dear that if she could have climbed off this horse and kissed him, she would have. Instead, she just listened.

"They said yes. The surgery was ugly. Recovery was harder. But then one morning, he got up on three legs and looked at me like, 'Well? You coming or what?'"

She laughed, picturing the sweet Irish setter and a teenaged Wade Reynolds.

"I built him ramps. I rigged this ridiculous homemade sling. He learned how to run again, just...differently. We got two years, three months, and two extra days of fun. They weren't perfect. But they were good. They were his."

She sighed, not entirely sure of the point, unless it was to make her fall harder for him. 'Cause that happened.

"That was the first time I really understood what I am," he said. "I'm not someone who fixes things because they're broken. I fix what's *between* someone and the life they want, for as long as they get to have it. I can't always change the ending—that's the curse of oncology. But I can change the middle."

"And that's what you wanted to do for me with all the...neuroscience and exoskeletons."

He shook his head. "Forget all that, Elise. I just want you to not be blocked from living your best life. Not normal, not better, not up to anyone's standards but yours. I swear."

"And the ramp and this saddle?" She lifted the reins.

"One of the very first things you told me was that you didn't love the process of multiple people helping and needing an escort. I started thinking about it then, called a buddy—"

"From college," she said on a laugh. "You have a lot of those."

"We 'bama boys stick together," he said. "But seriously, I wanted to solve that problem for you. And about all the things I suggested last night? If I could go back and smack myself upside the head, I would."

"You're a doctor," she said faintly. "You should know smacking yourself upside the head is never the answer."

He laughed, then looked very serious. "I'm sorry, Elise. I am so, so sorry. I don't want to fix you. I want to make your life better. A ramp? Easy. A harness? Simple. My heart? It's...yours."

She stared at him as a tear slipped free and warmed her cheek as it trickled down. "It is?"

"If you'll take it." He held her gaze with one so steady and sincere, it took her breath away. "I want the chance to spend however long you'll have me moving obstacles, not because you're broken, but because I'm crazy about you."

Copper shook his head as if he heard—and liked—every word. Elise reached to stroke his neck, needing something solid under her hand.

She could push Wade away. She could tell him the risk was too big, that long-distance residences and careers and the unpredictability of her own body made this a bad idea. She had built a life on being practical, on adjusting to what was left after the accident, on not asking for too much.

But here she was, up on a horse by herself on

Christmas morning because this man refused to let her fear be the only voice in the room.

"Okay, Dr. Reynolds," she said, steadying her breath. "Climb up."

His eyebrows shot up. "Excuse me?"

"Is there room for two in this contraption?"

He popped off the fence, landing with a thud. "There is now."

"Then let's ride...cowboy."

He chuckled, secured his hat, slipped her foot from the stirrup and replaced it with his own. In one graceful move, he swung his leg over.

He settled carefully behind her, keeping most of his weight off until he was sure the saddle could take it. It did. Copper stood solid, as if two people riding him on Christmas morning was the most normal thing in the world.

Wade's chest warmed her back. His thighs framed her hips, his arms coming around either side to lightly hold the reins with her.

It was the first time they were body to body, the first time she felt the whole of him pressed against her. It was...dizzying.

"Tell me if this is too much," he murmured near her ear.

"Too much what?" she joked, leaning back into him deliberately, feeling the way he sucked in a breath. "Too much goodness? Too much perfection? Too much Wade Reynolds? I honestly don't think there is such a thing."

Laughing, he kissed her hair.

"Now, Dr. Fix-It, let go of the reins," she ordered. "I've got them."

"Yes, ma'am," he said, and there was more than a little awe in his voice as he rested his hands lightly on her waist instead.

She clicked her tongue and flicked the reins, and Copper started walking forward. They paused at the paddock gate and he lifted the latch, letting her lead them out for the first time she'd ever left the enclosure on horseback.

The first time she ever felt a man against her. The first time she fell in love.

Lots of firsts for Elise Hale this Christmas morning.

She let out a giddy giggle, looking up at the clouds in the sky to thank whoever ran this world. He'd just worked a miracle.

"Hey, Elise?" Wade said quietly in her ear.

"Hmm?"

"Will you be my girlfriend?" The question was simple, almost boyish, threaded with humor and something very real. "Officially. So when people ask why I'm hanging around Utah grinning like an idiot, I can give them a respectable answer."

Her heart swelled so full she wondered how it stayed inside her ribs. She turned as far as the saddle and her body would allow, reaching up to loop an arm around his neck. It wasn't the smoothest maneuver in the world—her hip strap tugged a little, Copper snorted in mild offense at all the shifting—but Wade steadied her easily, one arm banded around her middle.

"You sure you're up for all the maintenance?" she asked, searching his face. "The ramps and the schedules and me getting mad when you try too hard?"

"I'm counting on it," he said. "And for the record, I don't see maintenance. I see...us. Figuring things out. Together."

He was close enough now that she could see the flecks of gold in his green eyes, the faint line on his chin from some long-ago mishap. With Murphy, no doubt. Snow dusted his lashes. He looked like every good decision she'd ever been too scared to make.

"Yes," she said. "I'll be your girlfriend."

His answering smile made her feel like the sun had come up inside her chest. Then he kissed her, properly this time, his mouth warm and sure and a little tentative at first, like he was giving her every chance to pull away.

She didn't. She finished the kiss, turned, and snapped the reins just like the cowgirl she really was.

Epilogue
MJ

MJ stood just beyond the Starling Room doors, smoothing her dress and breathing in the scent of pine, champagne, and the bonfire crackling outside. Inside, the band eased into a slow, drifting melody, and laughter rose and fell like a tide against Snowberry Lodge's sturdy bones.

Nicole and Cameron had danced their last dance only moments ago, glowing with that just-married light that made everyone around them a little warmer. Elise's toast—equal parts tearjerker and laugh out loud comedy—had guaranteed that every guest ruined their mascara and got a new laugh line.

Beaming with pride, Cindy and Jack looked ten years younger, leaning into one another as if remarriage had turned back time.

MJ pressed her hand to her chest, feeling overwhelmed by a fresh dose of optimism, her drug of choice. So much love in one room. So much joy and family and hope.

There'd been a time when all of those things had seemed far away. When Cindy and Jack divorced. When their mother died, and then the darkest of time when she lost George. Just a year ago, when they flirted with a scam that almost wiped them out, then scraped by in December only to have the roof cave in—literally.

It was all so tenuous and terrifying until a certain Graham Matthew Walker appeared in her life and—

"Well," a familiar voice murmured behind her, rich and warm as mulled cider. "That was about the prettiest wedding I've ever seen."

She smiled and turned to look into Matt's eyes, sighing at the sight of him all relaxed, with his tie loosened, his cheeks touched pink from dancing and a little champagne.

Her heart did that flutter thing that was so frequent she was used to it now, just looking at him.

"It was perfect," she said, slipping into his arms. "And I'm so glad you were here."

His smile deepened. "I kind of feel like I belong. How'd you manage that?"

She gave a small, breathy laugh. "I didn't do anything but...love you."

"Same, Mary Jane," he whispered, brushing a kiss to her temple. "Same."

Together, they swayed to the faint music drifting from inside, his arms circling her from behind, their bodies moving as though the night had slowed to honor this one moment.

From where they stood, she could see Gracie and Marshall slow-dancing near the Christmas tree, wrapped in their own world. Beyond them, Benny and Olivia darted in and out of clusters of guests—first whispering to

Nicole, then tugging at Jack, then darting back toward the door like undercover elves on a mission.

"What are those two up to?" MJ murmured.

"Probably nothing you want to know about," Matt said lightly.

"Oh, heavens. Where's Red?"

"Avoiding Bertie, who is trying to convince the DJ to put on a line dance that she could lead with Red."

MJ snorted. "She's leaving tomorrow and my father will be free."

"I think he'll miss the attention." He gave her a squeeze. "Grab the pretty fur wrap and take a walk with me?"

"Now?"

"Yes, now. It's almost midnight and we should be able to see the Park City fireworks from the gazebo."

"Oh. That sounds nice."

They slipped out, passing the coat rack to grab the black faux fur she'd worn earlier for a few outside pictures. Stepping into the moonlight, their breath turned to clouds as they followed the dozens of soft lanterns that lit the grounds for the wedding night festivities.

"Are you warm enough?" he asked, glancing over his shoulder as if he expected someone to be behind them.

"Perfect." Honestly, she was glowing too much inside to feel the cold.

He guided her down the snowy path toward the gazebo—the one they'd built for summer weddings but ended up using all year round.

Tonight, the white wood structure looked like a

festive wedding cake—topped with snow, trimmed with garlands, alive with lights draped from the circular roof. The tall pine next to it was laden with more lights, making the whole gazebo as bright as a stage.

A table to the side held what looked like two fresh champagne flutes, full to the brim, but when she paused to consider what to do with them, Matt gave her a tug.

"No busing the tables tonight, MJ."

She agreed with a laugh, letting him lead her up the few steps into the gazebo.

"We wouldn't have this if not for you," she mused, gesturing to the precious structure nestled under the mountains.

He waved it off and turned her so her back faced the lodge. "I think this is where we'll see the best fireworks," he said, glancing over his shoulder again, then looking down at her. "Yep. Best view in Utah, after all."

She laughed, flattered as always, but he was acting a teeny bit...tense? That wasn't like Matt, but he did seem a little odd.

"Is everything okay?" she asked, searching his face.

"It will be," he said cryptically.

"What does that—"

He hushed her by taking both her hands, his thumbs brushing along her knuckles. The lantern light caught in his eyes, softening them, deepening them.

"Mary Jane," he said quietly, "there's something I need to tell you."

The serious tone made her heart lurch. "Okay...tell me."

He hesitated, gaze darting over her shoulder as though checking something. "I, uh, don't really know how to say this."

Her heart plummeted. "Just tell me, Matt. Anything. Don't drag it out."

"I have to..." He looked over her shoulder again, then twice, and instinctively she started to turn but he gripped her shoulders and refused to let her move. "I don't want to look at houses anymore," he said so quickly she wasn't sure she heard him.

Her breath snagged. "You don't?"

"No." He squeezed her shoulders, holding her with his gaze and a light grip. She thought she heard something behind her—a whisper, maybe a footstep—but she couldn't turn. Not now. She was fully focused on Matt, and it was probably a caterer who'd come to get the discarded champagne.

"I've figured out where I want to live," he said.

"Where?" Her voice was small, a little afraid but only because he sounded so uncertain. "Am I going to hate this? Am I going to be sad because wherever you're going, I can't because...I live here?" She let out a sad moan. "I'm sorry, Matt, but I can't leave Snowberry Lodge. I just can't—"

He looked behind her again, his eyes flickering as if he were not listening to her at all, but was more concerned with the lodge.

"Okay, okay," he said. "We're good now."

"Excuse me?" She realized the hands that held her

were trembling slightly. "Matt? What is going on with you?"

"Before I tell you where I'm going to live, I need to... well, I need to ask you something first."

She closed her eyes, knowing what was coming. He wanted her to move or travel or...it didn't matter. She wasn't going to do that, but she did love him, so surely they could work something out.

"Go ahead, Matt. Ask me...anything."

His lips curled up. "Anything?"

"Anything at all. I give you my word, I will answer you honestly."

He took a very deep breath and one more glance behind her, a twinkle in his eyes. "Okay, then." A nervous laugh escaped him as he slid his hands over the fur wrap, down her arms, taking her bare, cold hands in his.

"MJ, you are the most hopeful person I've ever met."

She didn't respond, but looked at him, completely uncertain where he was going.

"I've never seen anyone face life the way you do," he continued. "Always believing in something good in the next breath. You've made my whole world lighter. Brighter. Honestly..." His voice thickened. "I know people think of me as a lottery winner, but you're the grand prize, MJ. I really won life's lottery when I met you."

Her throat tightened. The air grew impossibly still. And suddenly, MJ was aware of...sounds behind her. Soft breathing, footsteps, some whispers, and the stretched silence of a whole bunch of people holding one collective breath.

What was—

He let go of one hand, reaching into his pocket as he very slowly lowered to one knee, looking up at her with nothing but love in his eyes.

Wait! *This* was happening?

Behind her, a wave of whimpers and gasps slipped through the night, and suddenly a semicircle of family and friends surrounded the outside of the gazebo.

Matt opened a small black box to display an antique diamond ring that glittered with every light in the gazebo.

"Mary Jane McBride," he said, voice steady and full, "you are everything I ever dreamed of and more than I could imagine. I would like to make your life happy, content, peaceful, and full. Will you marry me and spend the rest of your life as my wife?"

Her hand pressed to her lips. Tears burned her eyes. Her knees wobbled and her heart stopped.

The world blurred except for him—this man, this miracle, kneeling in the snow and asking her to be his home. Did it matter where they lived?

No. Nothing mattered but saying the only thing she could say.

"Yes," she whispered, breathless before she cleared her throat to make sure everyone he'd secretly gathered as witnesses really heard her. "Yes, of course I will!"

Matt surged to his feet, pulling her into his arms as the group that surrounded them erupted with a cheer.

He kissed her and then slipped the ring on her finger, both of them laughing and crying at the same time.

When he finally loosened his hold, she pressed her forehead to his, laughing through tears.

"You said you knew where you wanted to live," she reminded him, breath hitching as she braced for his answer. "Where?"

He pointed toward the lodge, up to the third-floor window glowing with warm light. "Home," he said simply. "Where you are. That's where I want to live."

She melted all over again.

Family poured into the gazebo—led by Benny and Olivia, who offered up the champagne glasses from the table, their eyes sparkling with the role they'd played in the surprise.

"Mom! Congratulations!" Gracie hugged MJ so hard she nearly lifted her off the gazebo floor.

Cindy was crying openly when she came in for her hug.

"Can you believe this?" MJ whispered to her sister.

"I believe you deserve the greatest love story imagin-able and I'm so happy for you."

"Oh, Cin. Thank you. I love you."

They hugged again while Jack clapped Matt's shoul-der. Nicole squealed and danced around, so beautifully willing to share her big day with her old aunt.

Red lumbered over and hugged her. "So happy for you, my dear daughter."

"Fifteen seconds to midnight!" Someone yelled.

More voices joined as a noisy countdown began.

"Ten...nine...eight..."

Matt wrapped his arm around MJ and leaned close. "I can't wait for you to be Mrs. Walker."

"Six...five...four..."

She closed her eyes and held onto the moment with both hands and her whole heart.

"Three...two...one..."

A chorus of "Happy New Year!" rang out just as the first firework shot into the winter sky, exploding in a spray of color and hope.

"Happy New Year," Matt whispered as he kissed her smiling lips.

Happy New Year, happy new life.

MJ had found her future and it was brighter and better than ever.

♣

LOOKING for another Christmas collaboration from Hope Holloway and Cecelia Scott? Enjoy a Carolina Christmas, a charming, heartwarming holiday series that will whisk you away to a dreamy winter in the Blue Ridge mountains.

Carolina Christmas by
Hope Holloway *&* Cecelia Scott

The Asheville Christmas Cabin
The Asheville Christmas Gift
The Asheville Christmas Wedding
The Asheville Christmas Tradition

If you're in the mood to bask in the sunshine of a gorgeous beach, fall in love with an unforgettable cast of characters, and get lost in stories you cannot put down... you've come to the right authors!

Other family saga beach reads by
Hope Holloway and Cecelia Scott

Hope Holloway

Coconut Key

Shellseeker Beach

Seven Sisters

Cecelia Scott

Sweeney House

Young at Heart

***

Collaborations by Hope and Cecelia

Carolina Christmas

The Destin Diaries

***

Visit www.hopeholloway.com and www.ceceliascott.com for
details about all of their books!

About The Authors

Hope Holloway is the author of charming, heartwarming women's fiction featuring unforgettable families and friends, and the emotional challenges they conquer. After more than twenty years in marketing, she launched a new career as an author of beach reads and feel-good fiction. A mother of two adult children, Hope and her husband of thirty years live in Florida. When not writing, she can be found walking the beach with her two rescue dogs, who beg her to include animals in every book. Visit her site at www.hopeholloway.com.

Cecelia Scott is an author of light, bright women's fiction that explores family dynamics, heartfelt romance, and the emotional challenges that women face at all ages and stages of life. Her debut series, Sweeney House, is set on the shores of Cocoa Beach, where she lived for more than twenty years. Her books capture the salt, sand, and spectacular skies of the area and reflect her firm belief that life deserves a happy ending, with enough drama and surprises to keep it interesting. Cece currently resides in north Florida with her husband and beloved kitty. Visit her site at www.ceceliascott.com